"A meeting of minds— that's a love affair?"

Carissa ignored his derision. "To want a man with my mind *and* my body is important—but I don't want any sort of love affair with you."

She twisted aside, but Cade touched the corner of her mouth gently with his, then slid his lips across hers, teasing, caressing. "Because I won't pretend that I love you?" he asked, his hand sliding down to slowly stroke her back.

She broke away. "No. Because you *don't* love me. Because you haven't loved any of the women in your life. To you women are just a procession of faces...."

"Once that might have been nearly true," he said slowly. "But not since eight years ago, when I first met you."

"That's a cheap lie," she choked. She knew the difference between lust and love. All the hurt of the past had taught her well.

Other titles by

DAPHNE CLAIR
IN HARLEQUIN ROMANCES

DAPHNE CLAIR

darling deceiver

Harlequin Books

TORONTO•LONDON•NEW YORK•AMSTERDAM
SYDNEY•HAMBURG•PARIS•STOCKHOLM

Harlequin Presents edition published May 1980
ISBN 0-373-10355-7

Original Hardcover edition published in 1980
by Mills & Boon Limited

Printed in U.S.A.

CHAPTER ONE

THE airline had mixed up the tickets somehow, and Cade was separated from his manager by the width of the narrow aisle. The hostess had offered to ask the other ticket-holder to change places, but when she said the lady was already seated, Cade said curtly, 'Never mind. It doesn't matter.'

He hated to have special treatment because of his blindness, even more than he enjoyed buying it because of his fame and the wealth it had brought him. When in doubt about the reasons, he would assume a connection with his disability, and pride often produced a harsh reaction.

Aware of Jack's warning hand on his arm as they proceeded down the plane to their seats, he tried to curb his irritation. Too much temperament was bad for his image, Jack always said, when he allowed his acid tongue to lash at someone who plainly pitied him for his disability. A certain amount of Latin fire was okay, but the fans must not be alienated. Sometimes Cade hated the whole business.

He was conscious of the woman beside him when he sat down. When the chatter in the cabin paused he heard the soft sound of her breathing, the click of her safety belt and the small sound of the clasp on her handbag as she opened it. Her arm brushed his sleeve lightly as she rummaged in the bag for something. She wore a light flowery perfume, not too heavily applied; the faint scent of it reached him now and then when she moved.

She had murmured some polite greeting when he sat down, which he had returned with nothing more than a slight, cold nod. Unreasonably, he was annoyed with

her over the seating muddle. It was going to be a
nuisance not having Jack beside him when the meal
came. He hated the thought of being made conspicuous
by having his manager cross the aisle to help him. Besides, this was one of those days when he was sick of
keeping up his public image. He hoped the woman on
the next seat had never heard of him.

The hostess touched his shoulder and said, 'Would
you fasten your seat belt, please, Mr Fernand. Do you
need help?'

'No, thanks.' She moved on, and he fumbled and
found the buckle and snapped it into place.

The woman beside him said, 'Excuse me, you *are*
Cadiz Fernand, aren't you?'

He contemplated denying it, but the voice had surprised him. It was a particularly pleasant one, low and
soft with a hint of huskiness, but clear and with a trace
of some accent he couldn't place. And he wanted to
hear it again. She wasn't American, but he didn't think
she was English, either. Probably Australian, he
guessed.

He nodded and turned his face to her—the famous
'sensuous Latin face' as some fool of a columnist had
once called it, with the proud nose and the bitter, beau-
tifully masculine mouth and the very dark glasses
covering equally dark blind eyes.

'I like your music very much,' she said.

He sighed inwardly and waited for the next line ('I
have *all* your records,' or 'I suppose everyone says
that!'), but it didn't come.

After a moment he said, 'Thank you.' And began to
like her a little better. After all, it wasn't her fault
about the seats.

After a while he went to sleep. He had done a show
in Honolulu the night before, and it was a long flight
to Sydney where he would be performing again tomorrow night.

He woke feeling dry-mouthed and uncomfortable. The woman was turning over the pages of a magazine, and with a return of his former irritation he wondered if that was what had woken him. The dry crackling got on his nerves.

He called 'Jack!' softly, and Jack was immediately beside him. 'Let's take a walk, do you mind?' Cade said.

'Sure, Cade—this way.'

Cade had liked Jack Benton from their first meeting. He had been quick to learn how to deal with a blind man, and had never acted as though Cade must be deaf, crippled and mentally retarded as well.

He returned to his seat feeling fresher, and ordered a drink. The woman politely refused an offer to join him. She offered to read him the menu, and he accepted, sipping at his cool drink and listening to the warmth of her attractive voice.

When the food came, he refused the stewardess's offer of help, and was relieved that Jack must have taken the hint, too. No presence hovered beside him as he carefully found the wrapped cutlery and removed plastic covers from the dishes. He managed the starter and the main course without difficulty, then groped for a spoon for the dessert, but a cool hand took his fingers and placed it in them.

He thanked her rather shortly, and she said, 'It had slipped down the side of the tray.'

He understood that she wouldn't have helped if she had thought he would find it quickly, and felt a little sorry for his curtness.

'My brother is blind,' she explained.

'I see.' He must have trained her well.

By the time their coffee cups had been removed he felt in a mood to listen to that attractive voice for a while. He turned and gave her the smile that made millions of hearts flutter.

'You have the advantage of me,' he said.

'I—have I?'

'You know *my* name,' he pointed out.

'Oh!' Her low, breathy laugh was rather attractive, too, he noted.

'Carissa Martin,' she said. 'Most people call me Crissy.'

'I like Carissa better,' he said. 'It's unusual.'

'My mother got it from a book.'

'Your mother had good taste.'

He asked about her blind brother.

'Clive is studying electronic engineering,' she said.

'Sounds pretty difficult,' he commented.

'It is,' she said. 'Even for a sighted person. I suspect that's one reason why he chose it. He's very determined, and I guess he feels he has something to prove.'

I guess he does, Cade thought. *Don't we all!* He felt some considerable empathy for the unknown Clive Martin.

'Are you Australian?' he asked.

'No, I'm a New Zealander. The accents sound similar to you Americans.'

'You sound almost English,' he said. 'Most Australians have a pronounced twang.'

'Oh, they don't all talk like Chips Rafferty,' she said. 'But I expect your ear is more acute than most.'

'Are you on your way home to New Zealand?'

'Yes, I've lived in the States for a year—it will be strange coming home.'

The plane shuddered and dropped a little, and he felt the small jarring as her hand clutched at the armrest beside him.

'Are you nervous?' He raised his own hand to cover hers, finding the skin smooth and warm under his fingers.

'Not terribly,' she said. 'I was a bit startled, that's all.

I haven't flown much, really. *You* must be quite used to it, I suppose.'

He thought she was more scared than she admitted, as the plane continued to shake intermittently. She spoke quickly and her voice had a suddenly breathless quality. The hand under his quivered a little and he tightened his long fingers on it, partly to reassure her and partly because he liked the feel of the smooth, silky skin against his palm. His thumb absently caressed her wrist as he said, 'Yes, I travel a lot. Mostly by plane. It's supposed to be the safest mode of travel, you know.'

'Yes, I had heard that.'

She still sounded faintly agitated, and he went on talking, his beautiful singer's voice deliberately soothing as he told her about some of the journeys he had made, the places he had seen.

When the plane flew out of the turbulence, she quietly withdrew her hand as they resumed a steady, even flight.

'I think I'll have a short nap,' she said.

'Have I bored you?'

'Oh, no! Please don't think that. You've been fascinating me, Mr Fernand. It was kind of you to try to take my mind off the plane, but you must be tired of talking to me.'

Surprised, he said, 'What makes you think that?'

'Well, you obviously didn't want to talk before— when you got on the plane. I expect you're tired after last night's performance.'

'Were you there?'

'I'm afraid not. I boarded in Los Angeles. And I'll miss your show in Sydney, too.'

'You're going straight on to New Zealand, then?'

'No. I have two days in Sydney. I'll be staying in a hotel with an aunt who lives in Adelaide. But your shows will be booked out, I'm afraid, before I get there.'

'I'll get Jack to leave two tickets at the box office for you. There'll be some kept for my friends.'

The genuine pleasure which warmed her voice when she thanked him convinced him she wasn't just being polite when she said she liked his music. Then, to his slightly piqued surprise, she lowered the back of her seat, and apparently did go to sleep.

When they stopped over at Nandi she left the plane, saying she wanted to buy a few souvenirs at the duty-free shop for her family and friends, and Jack crossed the aisle and sat beside Cade until she returned.

When he made to relinquish the seat to her, she said, 'Oh, no, please stay there. I don't mind taking your seat.'

Cade's own annoyance surprised him by its strength. Only a few hours ago he would have welcomed the change, but now he found he wanted that soft voice beside him, and he answered Jack's enthusiastic comments on the likely success of the Australian tour with little enthusiasm of his own. In his mind he was creating a mental picture of Carissa Martin.

After they left the plane he asked Jack what she was like.

'Nice,' Jack said, meaning good-looking. 'Very nice. Blonde, long hair but done up on top. Young, but stylish. A lady, you might say. Yeah—very nice. Wish I was twenty years younger.'

Cade brushed that remark aside. 'Eyes?' he said.

'Mm—darkish, I think. But not brown. Grey, maybe? Hazel? I dunno. Say, are you interested?'

He means, *do you want to sleep with her? Shall I fix it?*

'No,' Cade laughed, and clapped his friend on the shoulder to cover a rare surge of angry disgust that he knew was unfair. 'No, not that much.'

But—if she came to the show ...

'I promised to leave some tickets for her for the

show,' he said casually. 'Remember it, will you?'

'Sure.'

And Jack would remember. Not that Cade would have forgotten it ...

It was a great show. The crowd went wild, which they told him was unusual here. He played on their feelings with his guitar and with his voice, and felt them swaying with the moods that he created for them. He played a number with a strong, primitive beat, and they clapped and stamped in time with the music. He sang a sad South American lament, and they hushed and he felt them grieving with him for lost loves and forgotten childhoods. He sang a love song for a beautiful woman that he had written, and every woman in the audience knew it was for her. Their soft sighs of passion almost feathered his skin as he sat apparently relaxed and intimate in the spotlight he couldn't see. Here, it didn't matter that he was blind. They were all in darkness and only he had light. He couldn't see, but how he could make them *feel*! He felt like a god.

At the end they called him back again and again, with cheers and whistles and stamping feet. After the second encore when he went into the wings, Jack said in his ear, 'She's here.'

'Who?' His audience was calling him again, like a lover, and like a lover he didn't want to come down yet from the sweet heights that he had taken them to.

'Carissa Martin,' said Jack. 'Say, do you know what her name means? Dearest little schemer! Is that weird?'

Jack had a book of names and their meanings that he was almost superstitious about. 'Cadiz Fernand' had been his invention. Cade went along with the stage name in public, but simply refused to answer to it in private.

'Yeah, well get her backstage, Jack,' he said, and

walked confidently back on to the bare stage, his arms lovingly outstretched to their ovation.

There seemed to be a remarkable number of people in his dressing room. He was introduced to several names and accepted all their congratulations. Some of the women kissed his cheek. They all twittered. He remembered Carissa's warm, sweet voice, and wondered where she was.

Then Jack took his arm. 'You remember Miss Martin, Cade.' And a cool, firm hand clasped his.

'Thank you for the ticket,' she said. 'I loved the show.'

He remembered there was an aunt. Just because he didn't want her to go, and the smooth hand in his fingers was already beginning to withdraw, he asked, 'Did your aunt enjoy it?'

'She couldn't come, after all. She's still in Adelaide, in bed with some virus that's going round. I only used one of your tickets.'

'You don't know anyone in Sydney?'

'I don't know anyone in the whole of Australia, except my aunt—and you.'

The hand moved out of his grasp with some determination, against the fractional tightening of his fingers.

'Don't go away!' he said. 'Jack!' And he turned to someone's insistent grasp on his shoulder, knowing he could trust Jack to make sure she stayed until all these superfluous people had gone.

He did, and got them a taxi to a place he recommended for a late supper. Jack always knew the best places to go within hours of arriving in any city in the world.

Carissa Martin was good to be with. She guided him while seeming to be simply holding his arm like any pretty woman out with a man. They were seated as he liked, side by side, so that he could feel her movements, and she read the menu to him quietly but let him order. And didn't talk too much. She questioned the waiter about one or two things on the menu, and Cade thought he detected admiration in the man's voice as he replied, the subtle difference of cadence that denoted a masculine reaction to feminine beauty. He smiled to himself with a glimmer of satisfaction. The envy of other men was a compensation for his blindness. Having beautiful women to show off in places like this, to share social occasions and sometimes his bed, was a way of scoring off men who had their sight. Cadiz Fernand was never seen with a plain woman.

When they had eaten, he brushed a hand lightly down her left arm and fingered the watch on her wrist.

'Is it marcasite?' he asked, feeling the small chips about the smoothness of the glass.

'No, gold.'

'With—not diamonds.' She wasn't a diamond type, he thought.

'No, they're emeralds. Small ones.'

'To go with your eyes?'

She laughed, a little selfconsciously. 'Well, that depends. My eyes change colour with my mood. Sometimes they're green. Especially when I'm angry. When I feel sentimental, or emotional, they go grey. Mostly, I guess you'd call them hazel.'

Hearing movement and a chink of glassware behind him, Cade turned.

'Waiter?'

'Yes, sir?' The man bent over them.

He turned his face towards Carissa. 'What colour are the lady's eyes?' He heard her small gasp.

'Grey, sir. Dark grey.'

'Thank you.' He smiled at her in triumph, wishing he could see her expression, and handed the man a note. 'Call a cab for us, would you, please.'

'That wasn't fair!' she protested as the man moved away from them. He still held her wrist, and she tried to pull away, but he tightened his fingers against her resistance.

'No, *you* were unfair,' he said quietly. His fingers found her pulse, beating just a shade fast, he thought. 'You told me something you wouldn't have told a sighted man, because you thought I couldn't use it.'

She went very still and silent for a few moments. Then she said, 'I'm sorry.'

'Don't be.' He raised her hand to his lips and then let it go. 'Let's wait outside, shall we?'

Outside the doorway he said, 'Is anyone about?'

'No. It's very late.' He felt her shiver against his arm on her waist.

'And dark?'

'Yes.'

'Good,' he said, and kissed her.

For an instant she was stiff, as though he had surprised her, and he thought cynically, *surely not!* But her lips were parted and soft under his, and in a very few seconds her body curved into his as he pulled her close, and she felt warm and willing.

He kissed her closely and long, then whispered, 'Shall I tell the driver to take us both to my hotel?'

She drew back suddenly in a startled movement. 'Do you mean—are you—— Oh, I can't. I'm sorry. Not to-night.'

Pulling her back to him, he kissed her hair and throat. He wondered if it was *can't* or *won't*. She seemed to be a free agent, and had admitted she knew no one in Sydney. So it was *won't*. He could try to change her mind. There was, he sensed, a quality of reserve about her. A one-night stand wasn't her scene, he guessed. Nor his, normally, come to that, but this girl was intriguing and powerfully attractive, and in two days their ways must part. If he could persuade her that it needn't be for ever ...

His finger tracing the line of her throat, he murmured, 'I have one more day here—so do you, don't you?'

She nodded, then said, 'Yes.' But he had felt the movement of her cheek against his hand.

'Can we spend the day together—and maybe—tomorrow night?'

'I don't know. I can't promise.'

'But you'd like to?' he insisted. His lips traced the line of her jaw, his hand moved down to sweet, rounded softness, but she withdrew quickly as she heard a car stop at the curb.

'The taxi,' she said, on a note of relief.

Inside the cab he tried to put his arm around her, but she moved away and he thought resignedly, *she doesn't like kissing in taxi-cabs*. That hint of reserve again. *But, dammit, we only have two days*. And she wasn't indifferent.

He moved his hand and found hers, the left one. There were no rings on it. He had hoped there wouldn't be. He spread her fingers on his knee and put his hand over them. 'I asked you something,' he reminded her.

'To spend the day with you?'

'And the night.'

'I'm not going to answer that one.'

She didn't sound at all coy. Most women would have. Cade wondered if she was going to tease. He thought from her voice that she had her head turned away from him and was looking out of the car window.

'No?' he said.

'No.'

She still had her head turned away, and it began to annoy him. 'Is the view so fascinating?' he asked sharply.

He felt the jerk in her fingers as her head turned quickly.

'I'm sorry!' she said. 'How did you know?'

Something her brother hadn't taught her, he thought. But perhaps she wasn't in the habit of looking the other way when she talked to her brother. It occurred to him that was the third time she had apologised to him tonight. It might have been irritating, but he found it a rather graceful habit.

'What about the first question, then?'

'I thought,' she said rather carefully, 'that you might prefer not to ask it again unless I said yes to the second one.'

He thought about that. She had been giving him an out—rather gallant. He acquitted her of teasing.

'Carissa, dearest little schemer,' he said, laughing softly. 'I will be very disappointed if you turn me down tomorrow night, but I just might bear it if you let me meet you tomorrow morning immediately after breakfast, and take you to lunch, and dinner, and supper.' She hesitated, and he added, 'Just a day out sightseeing —no strings, I promise.'

He felt her suddenly relax, and she said, 'I'd love to. I really would love to!'

He hired a cab for the day, over Jack's protests that they had things to do, even though there was no show that evening.

'You're the manager,' said Cade. 'Go ahead and manage. I'm taking a day off, I'm resting. And Jack, do me a favour. Make yourself very scarce tonight, will you?'

'Carissa Martin? Look, Cade, do you know what you're doing?'

'I know what I'm doing!' Cade snapped. He supposed Jack was worrying about that ridiculous name of hers. 'Just get lost tonight and let me do it, will you?'

'But, Cade——'

'But nothing. I'll see you tomorrow, Jack.'

He took her to the Blue Mountains, a longish drive that gave them time to talk, in between her brief descriptions of the scenery.

'Why did you call me a little schemer, last night?' she asked him.

'Dearest little schemer,' he said. 'It's the meaning of your name. Didn't you know?'

'No!' she exclaimed. 'Is it? I don't believe it!'

'But it is!' He told her about Jack's book of names and the importance he attached to it. 'Jack says names are important, especially in show business. At one time. he wanted me to call myself Estebanito. He said it had a good ring to it. I think he'll always regret someone else thought of Engelbert Humperdinck before he did.'

She laughed and said, 'But your name is your own, isn't it?'

'Near enough,' he told her, and changed the subject.

Carissa described the muted sunset colours of the landscape to him as they passed, and the looming bulk of the mountains as they approached and began to climb. She told him how the peeling silvery bark of the gum trees looked in the sun, and when they got out she picked some of the blue-green leaves for him to rub in his fingers and sniff the pungent eucalyptus scent, and he ran his hand over the peeling bark for himself.

As they drove further up into the mountains the driver became talkative, telling them tales of the bush fires that periodically ravaged the countryside, and were always a danger in the summer when the temperatures climbed into the nineties and the dry trees needed only the smallest spark to ignite. 'Some families have rebuilt their homes three times,' he said. 'They just keep coming right back after every fire.'

'Why don't they live somewhere else?' Cade asked,

finding it hard to imagine such stubborn stupidity.

'They say it's home, and they'd never live anywhere else.'

'They'd have to start all over again each time,' said Carissa.

'Yeah—I reckon,' the driver agreed. 'But some of them are just so glad to be alive, I guess that seems a small thing, after all. Last fires up here, one family spent three hours in their swimming pool, with wet blankets over their heads, while their home just burned down practically round their ears. The fires simply swept right over them, they said.'

Carissa spoke again. 'I remember, a few years ago when there was a big fire over here, in New Zealand we had beautiful sunsets for days—especially spectacular, I mean. It was the haze from the smoke drifting from Australia that caused them.'

The driver whistled in surprise. 'Is that so? Clear across the Tasman, eh?'

'How far is that?' Cade asked.

Carissa answered, 'About thirteen hundred miles.'

He brushed a hand against her arm and said softly, 'Not very far by today's standards—by plane, for instance.'

There was a tiny silence before she said, 'No. But it's still a long way for smoke to drift.'

The driver was apparently still listening, because he interjected with an awed, 'Sure is! Jeez! Clear across the Tasman, eh?'

Carissa, sitting close to Cade's shoulder, quivered a little, and he wished he could see her smile.

The driver's manner to her amused Cade by its contrast to the waiter's admiration last night. The man had a hearty Australian twang and spoke to Cade with what passed in this egalitarian society for respect, and to his companion in a slightly avuncular way. Occasionally he hesitated over an adjective, and Cade guessed he was guarding his language for Carissa's benefit.

When he and Carissa got out again to walk for a while he said, 'Tell me if I've got our driver right. Late fifties—heavy-built, a bit overweight?'

'Very good!' she congratulated him. 'Also a moustache and thinning hair.' She paused, and tightened her grip on his arm. 'There are stones on the ground here. Watch your step.' They walked a little further and found a seat to rest on. Carissa described a panoramic view of the mountains backed by a blue-hazed sky, and fresh breezes blew the scent of the trees to Cade's nostrils.

'Are you always so good at guessing how people look?' she asked him.

Smiling, he said, '*You* are blonde, about five foot five, green-eyed——' he ignored a small disparaging exclamation from her, and went on. 'About—twenty-two? Twenty-three? Twenty-one?' he paused, and then laughed at her continued silence. 'You're not going to tell me. Am I close?'

'You're close,' she said. 'Don't you know it's not done to expect a woman to reveal her age?'

'You don't need to worry about that until you're nearer my age,' he told her.

'Thirty?' she said. 'But it doesn't matter for a man, does it?'

'So you know my age.'

'Of course. I'm a fan, I've read all about you.'

'Okay,' he challenged her. 'What else do you know?'

'You were born in Mexico. Your mother was from an old Spanish family, and they disapproved of her marrying your father, so they ran away to get married. Your father was a naturalised American, and you were born an American citizen, after they went to the States. You have a younger sister, but your father died when you were four years old. He left you a guitar, and by the time you were sixteen you were supporting your mother and sister playing in cafés. You were discovered by——'

'Okay, okay!' he stopped her. 'You're a fan! I believe you.'

'Didn't you believe me on the plane? Or when I came to the show?' she asked. 'I told you how I loved your music.'

'I was waiting for you to tell me that you have all my records.' He grinned at her, not his famous smile, but a look few people had seen, of pure enjoyment. 'What are you laughing at?'

'I *have*!' she said, still laughing. 'Every last one! Cross my heart, I have!'

He stood up, pulling her to her feet, and something soft and fine blew across his face. He touched her shoulders and held them in his hands. 'You've left your hair loose,' he said.

'Yes.'

He moved his hand to touch it. It came past her shoulders, and was soft in his fingers.

'It makes you look younger,' he said positively.

'What? How can you possibly know——?' She gave a soft, puzzled laugh.

'I know. I know by the way men react to you. It's different.'

'Is it?' she asked uncertainly. 'But it can't make any difference to you.'

He tightened his grip a little on the strand of hair he held, and moved it to tilt her face for his kiss, surprised and a little angry when she made a small movement of resistance, as though she had thought better of inviting it.

He wouldn't let her get away with it, because she must have known that her remark had provoked his action. He slid his free hand to her waist to pull her against him, and if his mouth was a little rougher than it might have been against her soft lips, she had herself to blame.

Perhaps the small punishment was more harsh than he had intended, because when he let her free her mouth from his she sounded almost frightened, pleading, 'Please—let me go!'

'Please, *Cade!*' he prompted, teasing her with faint cruelty, but wanting to hear her say his name in that lovely voice of hers.

'Please, Cade,' she whispered, beginning to struggle, her hands against his chest. 'Someone's coming.'

For a moment he didn't believe her. Then he heard the muted sound of footsteps and approaching voices, and let her go.

They stood above a deeply cleft valley and she told him about the stark standing grey rocks called 'The Sisters' that brooded over it. Then they rode across the valley in a swaying cable car, and she started to describe the view below, then suddenly clutched him in panic and refused to look any more.

This time when he kissed her he was more gentle at first, beginning with comfort rather than passion. But when they emerged at the other side of the valley she was satisfactorily breathless, and not from fear.

Cade paid off the taxi driver at her hotel and waited in the lobby while she changed. Then they went to his hotel and up to his suite while he showered and changed for the dinner they planned to have in the downstairs restaurant.

Coming out of the bedroom, he asked, 'Will you check this tie for me, Carissa?'

'It looks fine.' Her voice came from the couch, and he walked over to her, thinking they could have a meal sent up, but she caught his hand and pulled herself up by it, turning towards the door. He pulled her back into his arms for a long and expert kiss, and murmured against her ear, as his hand found her rapid heartbeat, 'Darling, are you staying with me?'

For a moment she didn't answer, and he moved his lips persuasively against her earlobe. 'Darling?'

She whispered, 'I brought my toothbrush. There's a large handbag on the couch beside me.'

Triumphantly, he kissed her again, smothering a slight sense of surprise. She was wearing something smooth and silky that left her shoulders and back bare, and rustled gently when she moved.

'I like this dress,' he said, his fingers tracing her shoulder blades, then moving to her waist.

'I thought you would.' Then she stirred in his arms. Her voice sounding a little shaky, she said, 'Cade, you promised me dinner, remember?'

She had a healthy appetite, and they lingered over their meal. Then they danced a little, closely, then he swept her back up to his suite and into his arms as soon as they closed the door, because she was stiffening up again. He could feel it in the arm pressed against his side, but he was damned if she was going to change her mind now.

It wasn't long before she was as warmly pliant against him as he could have wished, her breath coming quickly and her cheeks warm between his hands as he explored her soft, parted mouth.

He turned her into the room, towards the couch, and groped on it for her bag. Handing it to her, he said, 'There's a robe on the bathroom door, if you want one.'

'I brought one,' she said shakily.

He hoped it didn't have buttons. He hated it when a woman came to bed all fastened up as though she had no intention of sharing it with a man.

It did have buttons, but she had left them undone and just fastened it with a belt tied in a bow. He was briefly amused that she had bothered. It was lacy and light, and slid silently to the floor when he took it off and pushed her gently on to the bed.

She was very responsive, very undemanding, and followed his lead completely, except for one moment when she gave a tiny shudder of withdrawal. He stopped and said, 'What is it?'

'It's all right,' she whispered. 'It's all right, truly,' and guided his hand back to where it had been.

He waited until he knew she was ready for him, so that her sudden rigid resistance took him completely by surprise, annoying him to ruthlessness. By the time he realised the reason for it, it was far too late. By then he was beyond thought, only feeling ...

He lay back beside her, and it was one of the bad times, when he wished like hell that he could see. His voice was harsh as he said, 'Why didn't you tell me you were a virgin?'

She didn't answer him, her breathing soft and so even he was sure she was consciously keeping it so. At least she wasn't crying.

A thought struck him like a blow over his heart, and he sat up and turned on her, groping until he found her shoulders, wanting to shake her. 'How old are you?' he said roughly.

'Twenty!' she said, sounding frightened. But this time he wasn't fooled. He shook her, then, fiercely, and repeated his question.

She sobbed just once and said in a defeated whisper, 'Seventeen.'

His fingers tightened on her soft flesh, because he knew that if his hands were free he would hit her, and he hated himself enough without that.

She said, '*Please!* You're hurting.'

He let her fall back against the pillow. 'God!' he said. 'You bloody little fool!'

He fumbled for his robe and the dark glasses and put them on. He had a long cold shower while his jumbled emotions sorted themselves into a cold hard fury.

When he went back into the bedroom she seemed to have fallen asleep. Probably cried herself into it, he thought, without pity. He put on some clothes and returning to the other room, felt in a drawer for some cigarettes, finding something else as well. 'Something with emeralds,' he had said to Jack. 'But not flashy.' It felt like just what he had ordered. And he would have something more to say to Jack in the morning. Why hadn't he said ... ?

He tried the clasp until he had mastered it, then dropped the box back in the drawer and put the bracelet in his pocket. He ran his fingers over the top of the desk until he located an ashtray, then took it to the couch and lit a cigarette.

There were six butts in the ashtray when he heard movement from the bedroom, and Carissa's voice said uncertainly, 'Cade?'

He got up and went in, and when his foot kicked against her robe on the floor he picked it up and tossed it to her. 'Here,' he said. 'Get up.'

He heard the bed move as she obeyed him.

'Can I use the bathroom?' she said.

'Be my guest,' he said sardonically.

She didn't move, and after a moment or two she said, 'It's dark. I can't see.'

Exasperated, he said, 'Come here,' and when she came close to him he took her arm and guided her to the bathroom, hearing the click of the switch as she turned on the light. Then he switched on the light in the main room and waited for her.

When she came out he was standing by the desk.

'Come here,' he said. She came close and he said, 'Give me your hand,' and when she hesitated he impatiently found her arm and slid his fingers down to her wrist and snapped the bracelet on to it. He lifted her hand to his lips because he always did at this stage, then dropped it.

Her voice shook as she asked, 'Did you buy this for me?'

'Of course. Don't you like it?'

'Yes, of course I like it. It's beautiful—thank you. But I can't possibly accept it.'

He heard the click of the clasp and then the small clatter as she placed it on the desk beside him, and her hair briefly brushed his cheek as she straightened. She smelled of soap and flowers, and suddenly his anger could be contained no longer.

'I'm sorry,' he drawled. 'I'd forgotten that young virgins come more expensive. But then I wasn't to know, was I?'

'*Cade!*' He heard the shock and pain in her voice with satisfaction. 'You're not *buying* me!'

'Oh yes, I am. I always buy my women, one way or another. It's one way of ensuring they're not motivated entirely by pity,' he said bitterly.

'I don't pity you. You know I don't. And I can't possibly take such a valuable present.'

'Why not? You've earned it.'

'Please don't, Cade.' No tears now. The voice that had fooled him with its husky maturity, was quiet and oddly dignified. 'Apart from anything else,' she added, wrecking the illusion instantly, 'how could I explain a gift like that to my parents?'

The reminder of how young she was stirred his anger again. He wanted to show her what a stupid child she was, completely out of her depth playing grown-up games.

'You'd think of something,' he said. 'You're a great little liar.'

'I haven't lied to you!' she cried. Then more quietly she said, 'I know you thought I was older, but *I* didn't tell you so.'

'You said I was close when I guesed your age at twenty-two or three.'

'Or twenty-one,' she reminded him. 'All right,' she said, as he remained silent, his mouth implacable, 'call it a lie. Is that why you're so angry with me? Because of one little lie?'

'Yes!' He almost shouted at her. 'One lie that any man with two good eyes in his head wouldn't have believed for two seconds!'

'Oh, Cade!' she protested on a tiny laugh. 'They would! Honestly they would. I look easily twenty.'

'You don't! Only with your hair up. And I doubt if you look eighteen even then. *You little cheat!*' he snapped viciously.

'I didn't mean to cheat you!'

'Well, you did. I wanted a woman for the night,' he told her, with a fine edge of insult, 'and I got a child.'

'I'm not a child!' She sounded stung. 'Everyone thinks I'm older. *You* did!'

'But not in bed, my dear!' he jeered softly. 'That's where we separate the women from the little girls.' He paused. 'Is that why you did it? Was I supposed to initiate you into womanhood?'

'No,' she said. 'I did it because *you* asked me.'

'How long have you been waiting for someone to ask?'

'That's terribly cruel.' Her voice shook, and he wondered if she was crying again. 'I wouldn't have—with anyone else. It was because it was you. I know you only wanted a girl for the night, but I've admired you so much, for so long. And now I've got to know you in person. I love you.'

Savagely, he said, 'You've known me for *two days*! So don't be so damned stupid!'

'I've known you much longer than that. I know a lot about you.'

'What you read in the magazines? Most of it's lies

made up by Jack or the writers. Even my name is a lie. You know *nothing* about me.'

'I do now.'

'Because you slept with me? Don't be silly.'

'I'm not silly! It doesn't matter if some of the stories are lies, or your name isn't the one you use on stage. I know you've worked to get to where you are, to over-come your handicap as well as all the other hurdles any singer has to clear. I know you can be kind and con-siderate, and—and sometimes cruel.'

'As a description of my character, it lacks something. All men are kind when they want it, and cruel after they've got it. Didn't you know?'

'I couldn't,' she said flatly. 'Could I?'

'Oh, that's right—it was your first time, wasn't it? My God, if I'd wanted a child-virgin I could have found one easily enough. They turn up every so often. Jack metaphorically spanks them and sends them home to their mothers. And why the hell he didn't do the same with you ...' A thought struck him, coldly, like an ice-cube down his spine, and he said, 'I don't sup-pose you used anything either, did you?'

'Wh-what?'

'Contraception!' he snapped. 'Did it occur to you that you might get *pregnant*, playing grown-up games?'

The way she stammered, he knew she must be blush-ing. '*Oh!* I th-thought that *you*—I mean, I hardly had a chance to—I was with you all day!'

He thought about the chances and decided it wasn't likely. But he hoped it would give her something to think about over the next few weeks. About as long as it should take him to shove her to the back of his mind.

'I'm sorry,' she muttered, sounding ridiculously humble, like a scolded child.

'What the hell were you doing, flying across the world on your own?' he demanded. 'What kind of parents have you got?'

'My parents are wonderful!' she said indignantly.
'They'd be horrified if they knew ... I was on an ex-
change scholarship in America,' she said. 'And they
thought my aunt was meeting me here. I told you.'

So the sick aunt did exist.

'I'm sorry,' she said again.

Irritated, Cade snapped, 'Oh, for God's sake!' And
turning from her, his outflung hand sent something
crashing on the desk beside them. His sleeve was wet
and he realised that someone had put a vase of flowers
there that hadn't been part of the desk furnishings
when he moved in. Cursing, he pulled out a handkerchief and dabbed at his sleeve, furious at the stupidity
of the hotel staff and his own clumsiness. He felt her
beside him, putting back the vase, rustling among the
flowers, trying to replace them, he supposed.

'Leave it!' he said irritably, and moved away from
her, roughly stuffing the handkerchief into his pocket.

She had moved, too, and he turned to the sound of
her voice. 'Would you like a towel?'

'No.' He ran a hand through his hair, trying to be
calm. He said, 'You could at least have told me it was
your first time.'

'Would it have made a difference?'

'Yes, dammit! It would. I probably wouldn't have—
taken you. A one-night stand is no way to lose your vir-
ginity.'

'I thought that men—that it was something special
for a man——'

Brutally, he said, 'My dear girl, collecting maiden-
heads is a pastime for college boys and ageing lechers.
My tastes are more sophisticated. Besides, it's well
known that virgins are no good in bed.'

Carissa went so still he thought she had stopped
breathing. Or she had moved while he was talking, and
left the room. He moved his head and couldn't sense
her near him. Had she gone?

Furious, he took several strides across the room without taking his bearings, and found himself standing and not knowing where he was, nothing within reach of his groping fingers. He didn't know which way he was facing, or if another step would bring him blundering against a chair or the coffee table or into a wall. Sickening panic gripped him, before he returned to sanity and said violently, '*Carissa!* Where the *hell* are you?'

Suddenly she was in his arms, and he automatically closed them round her as she cried softly, 'I'm here, Cade. I'm sorry! It's all right, I'm here!'

He put his face on her soft hair and held her tightly, wiping away her tears with his fingers, and poignant bitterness filled him at the thought of the dawn breaking outside.

CHAPTER TWO

CARISSA jumped from the trolley-bus and walked quickly along Auckland's Queen Street and around the corner into a relatively quiet side lane. The lobby of the tall building where she worked was deserted, and she had the elevator to herself as it whisked her silently to the fifth floor.

She crossed the cushioned vinyl of the corridor to the door marked *Morris Carey Wyatt: Entertainment for New Zealand* in discreet black and gold lettering, and entered the carpeted offices where she had worked for the last five years, since she was barely twenty.

She said good morning pleasantly to the girl behind the desk where she herself had started with Morris Wyatt, entrepreneur extraordinary, the man everyone in the business credited with putting New Zealand's small islands on the map as far as overseas entertainers were concerned.

Now Carissa had a small office all her own, and the title of personal assistant to Morris, with a salary to match. She was something more than a super-secretary —more, she told him somewhat dryly once; a super-dogsbody. It was her job to find any loose ends Morris left and tie them up, to deputise for him when he wasn't available, to keep the business wheels oiled and make sure the machine still ran when he was away, as he had been, on a flying visit to Australia, over the last few days.

The girl's voice stopped her as she was about to enter her office. 'Mr Wyatt is waiting for you, Miss Martin.'

'He's back?' She had known his plane would be here early this morning, but hadn't expected him back in the office before noon. His trips tended to be hectic, and usually he went to his flat and snatched a few hours' sleep before he came back to work, sure of a clear head and a keen eye. Not that she had ever seen Morris less than bright-eyed and bushy-tailed. He had the energy of a minor hurricane, but a much better sense of direction. She admired the man tremendously.

'He said he wants to see you the minute you get in, Miss Martin.'

'Oh—thank you, Sandra.'

Carissa changed direction and went down the short passageway to Morris's office, wondering what was up, her gaze automatically flicking over the row of famous faces whose photographs relieved the plainness of the white wall. All of them represented well-known overseas acts which Morris had brought to New Zealand at some time, a few of them more than once. Quite a lot of well-known entertainers toured Australia, and Morris had made it his business—almost a mission in life— to persuade them that a short trip across the Tasman sea would repay the time, effort and expense. He had been a bit cagey about just what his aim had been this trip, but Carissa knew that one or two celebrity musical stars were expected in Sydney within the next few months, and guessed he hoped a personal approach might secure some talent for the New Zealand scene. He had good contacts with some of the Sydneyside agencies. Perhaps he had arranged a short-notice concert or tour and wanted to make some fast arrangements. Booking venues, advertising, printing tickets—there would be a million things to do . . .

He was standing at the window when she walked in, rubbing reflectively at his chin, which meant he was worried or possibly baffled about something. Morris was a big man with a thick black moustache that matched his hair which he wore long enough to cover his shirt collar, and bright blue eyes that never missed a trick if there was likely to be money or entertainment in it.

'I didn't expect you back so soon,' she greeted him. 'Sandra said you wanted to see me straight away. She made it sound urgent.'

He waved vaguely at a chair, and she sat down and waited.

'I want you to do something for me,' he started, moving restlessly away from the window, but not sitting down.

'That's what you pay me for, Morris,' she answered humorously. 'What is it this time? Have you booked a temperamental act? Someone needing oodles of patience and Tender Loving Care?'

He grinned, but a little uneasily. 'That's part of it. You're awfully good at looking after the difficult cusses. But there's a bit more to it this time. It's a sort of unusual assignment.'

She liked unusual assignments, it was one of the good things about her job that the unexpected cropped up quite often, and she enjoyed the challenges it offered. But she felt a stirring of trepidation mixed with curiosity, because Morris didn't seem to think she was going to like this one.

'Well, what's it all about?' she asked.

'First of all,' he said. 'This is terribly confidential—in fact it could be a matter of life and death, literally, if you breathe a word.'

Carissa blinked and said, 'I won't, then.'

'And you're at liberty to refuse to do this, because it's—er—well, strictly speaking, it's not what you're paid for, I suppose. But I hope you will, because I know I can trust you, Carrie. You're discreet and levelheaded and extremely competent, and this job needs someone like you. Also you're unlikely to lose your head over the guy, which might be an advantage.'

'You're being very mysterious,' she smiled. 'Who is

the guy? One of the world's sex symbols, by the sound of it!'

'I guess he is. He's a singer—I don't want to name names——' He glanced about the room as though it might contain hidden microphones, making her smile inwardly. Whatever all the mystery was about, she suspected that Morris was rather enjoying it.

'Basically,' he said, in a low, confidential voice, 'I just want you to look after him, for a few days—maybe a few weeks. You've done it before, but this time it'll possibly be a bit longer than usual. And—well, there's a risk. It could be dangerous.'

'Why?' Joking, she said, 'I don't know any homicidal singers, do I?'

'*He* isn't homicidal. He's being threatened.'

'Threatened? You mean someone wants to kill him?'

'Someone *tried*, when I was in Aussie. But they don't know he's here—I hope. The thing is, he's got to lie low for a while, and someone has to nursemaid him. You, Carrie—please?'

Barely able to assimilate such bizarre facts, Carissa asked, 'Do I carry a gun?'

'*This is serious!*' Morris hissed.

'Sorry. Of course it is—if someone really tried to kill him, and it isn't just hoax threats. It isn't a publicity stunt, is it?'

'No, definitely not. I know his agent and his manager. No, this is for real, Carrie. Look, you can say no if you like. It isn't what you're paid for, but the plan needs someone absolutely trustworthy.'

'I'm flattered!'

'No, you're not. Flattery never got a man anywhere with you. That's another reason for picking you.'

Before she could work out an appropriate response to that, he said, 'Look, will you give me a yes or no, and then if it's yes, we can continue this discussion in my car.'

She thought for five seconds, then said, 'Yes. Why in your car?'

'I'll explain on the way,' he said, relief all over him. 'Come on.'

Barely five minutes later they were in his car, on the route to his suburban flat, and as they passed the grey neo-Gothic tower of the university on one side, and the stately green trees of Albert Park with its memorial statue of Queen Victoria on the other, Carissa said, 'You *are* going to explain all this, I hope?'

'Well, this thing blew up while I was there. Naming no names'—(he *was* really rather enjoying all this cloak and dagger stuff, Carissa thought)—'our lad is well known in America. Apparently there'd been some notes, telephone calls etcetera before he left for the Australian tour he's just completed. They figured once he left the country he'd be safe, and by the time he got back it would probably have died off of its own accord. But he got attacked—fortunately not hurt badly— when he was in Melbourne. His manager and agent called in a detective agency when the police seemed to draw blank, and came up with a plan—with which,' he said carefully, 'I offered to help. I'd been trying to get some New Zealand engagements for this guy, and I figured—well, if I help them out, they've got to be grateful, right?'

'Oh—right!' said Carissa. 'So, what was the plan?'

'The manager and all the rest of the party flew to the states as planned, on schedule—and *he* came home quietly with me.'

'He came home *with* you? He's—at your flat, now?'

'Right. That's why I want to get back there as soon as possible. I don't think anyone could have spotted him, but I don't mind telling you I'm nervous.'

'How long are you planning to hide him in your flat?'

'Only until tonight. You're going to the lodge.'

'The lodge.' Carissa was thoughtful. Kamahi Lodge
was a place they used occasionally as a quiet retreat for
celebrities wanting a few days' peace between engagements. It was on the shore of a beautiful inland lake,
surrounded by rugged bush country, the only neighbours a small motel nearby, and the fishermen who occupied for a few weeks at a time some of the huts scat-
tered about the shores of the lake. It should be safe
enough. On the other hand, if they *were* found there,
what chance did they have of getting help?

'Morris,' she protested, 'I'm not a bodyguard.'

'Don't worry,' he said. 'There'll be bodyguards, laid
on by the detective agency. You're going along to pro-
vide cover—and be chief cook and bottle-washer.'

Carissa sat up, a glint in her eye. 'You mean I'm
nothing but a cheap housekeeper!'

'Cheap? On *your* salary?'

'I'm worth every cent of it, Morris, and you know
it!'

'I do, I do!' he assured her hastily. 'Believe me, if I
could find a cook/housekeeper I could trust as I
trust you, I'd send her along.'

'I *hate* cooking!'

'But you do it, don't you? Now, don't go all Women's
Lib on me, there's a dear. Carrie, I *need* you!'

'Oh, all right,' Carissa sighed. 'But I don't fancy act-
ing cook to your beefy bodyguards as well as nursemaid
to your terrified singer.'

'Oh, he isn't terrified,' said Morris. 'He's mad as
hell! He'd like to wade in there and fight the whole
battle himself, if the police and his agent and his manager hadn't practically tied him down and made him
see sense.'

'I can see it's going to be one happy holiday!' Carissa
sighed.

'By the way, I don't think you'll have to cook for the
bodyguards. The idea is they'll be posing as huntin',

shootin' fishin' types using the nearest fishing hut—
the one by the lodge gates, near the road, so they can
monitor any callers. You and—er—our client will have
the lodge to yourselves. Looks better that way, in case
anyone's nosy.'

'My parents wouldn't have thought so,' Carissa murmured, as that sank in. 'What do you mean, better?'

'Well, for the record, in case anyone asks—you're
supposed to be a honeymoon couple. It'll explain why
you're not seen about much, you see.'

'I see.' Carissa digested that silently. She supposed it
made sense. Her parents wouldn't have liked it, but they
had both died four years ago in a car crash. And Clive,
her brother, was living in Invercargill, in the South
Island. Not that he would care if he had known. They
had a good relationship, but never interfered in each
other's lives.

As Morris drew the car into the carport in the court-
yard of his smart, exclusive town house, she asked, 'How
long are we supposed to stay at the lodge?'

'Well, the idea is for the bloke who's got his knife
into our boy to show his hand, and let the police nab
him. With any luck, he'll think his target is back at
home, and—well, it depends how long they take to
catch him. I'll keep in touch with you. I'm to be kept
informed at once of any new developments.'

'In other words, it could be days—or weeks? I hope
our—client—isn't going to stay "mad as hell" all that
time.'

'So do I, dear. That's your job—to keep him sweet.
I want him to do a tour for me some time.'

As Carissa went beside him to the door she said,
'Morris, I hope you haven't given this singer a notion
that it's my job to "keep him sweet". Some of them get
the wrong idea about that sort of thing.'

He looked reproachfully at her. 'Would I do that to
you? What the two of you do—or don't do—is your

business, personal business. I told him my personal assistant would be looking after him—and that's all.'

'But he knows about this plan of posing as a honey-moon couple?'

'Well—yes.'

'Then I'd like it to be clear that I'm not expected to do more than cook and—housekeep.'

'Sure, Carrie.' He opened the door to the flat and said, 'I'm sure you'll make it very clear.'

The room they entered was empty, but curtains blew softly at the open sliding glass doors to the terrace at the other side, and a pair of feet and a glimpse of knife-pleated trousers indicated someone lounging on one of the comfortable deck-chars outside in the sun.

As they crossed the room Carissa plucked at Morris's sleeve, murmuring, 'Aren't you going to tell me who it is?'

'No names,' he hissed back mysteriously. 'But you'll know when you see him.'

Resignedly, she followed him into the sun. The man rose swiftly even before they stepped out on to the little terrace, and she thought he might not be terrified, but he wasn't taking chances, either.

He was tall and dark, and the sunglasses he wore hid his expression, but she would have known him any-where—anywhere in the world. That face had haunted her dreams for years, and for a moment she was con-vinced this was another nightmare. The whole rather fantastic sequence of events seemed to lend credence to the idea.

Then Morris was holding her arm, pulling her for-ward, and saying, 'This is my personal assistant, Carissa Martin. Carrie—ere *Cade Franklin*.' His meaningful look, and the emphasis he put on the name were meant to convey it was a pseudonym, of course, but she didn't need them, and he must have known it. She hadn't even known that Cadiz Fernand was in Australia. For years

she had effectively developed a technique of simply not
reading anything in which his name appeared, of skip-
ping over headlines containing it, of switching off at
least mentally when anyone mentioned it. Of course,
she couldn't avoid sometimes seeing his picture, or hearing his music, but as far as one can block a world-
famous personality out of one's life, she had done it
with him.

She didn't know she had put out her hand until she
felt his strong fingers close around it, and his voice
saying calmly, 'Hello, Miss Martin. I've been hearing
about you from Morris. He says there isn't a more
competent, charming and discreet personal assistant
to be found.'

'Thank you—Mr Franklin.' For the life of her she
couldn't manage another word.

Morris said, 'How about drinks?' And she said, like
a person offered water in the desert, 'Oh, yes *please*,
Morris,' and sank into the nearest chair, a cushioned
coolie chair opposite the lounger that Cade had risen
from, and that he now returned to, but keeping his
feet on the ground as he sat sideways.

She felt a little strange, but the hope that she was
dreaming was fading every second. Cade hadn't
changed much, but the small increase in the width of
his shoulders, the few silvery hairs that glinted in the
sun just at the temples, the more pronounced firmness
of a mouth that had always held a trace of bitterness,
that now held a hint of implacability most of the time
instead of now and then, were real. The power and
attraction that emanated from him, even offstage, were
not the stuff of dreams.

She wished Morris would hurry back with the drinks.
All small talk had deserted her. She should be chatting
easily, putting the man at ease—as if he needed it. He
looked quite relaxed, sitting back against the cushions

of the lounger, arms loosely folded, eyes hidden behind those enigmatic glasses.

Then she received the second shock of the day. He
put up his hand and took the glasses off, and looked
at her, a rather leisurely and thorough look, from her
blonde hair, pulled back off her face into a soft French
pleat, over her lilac pink blouse and flared skirt, to her
slim ankles and high-heeled shoes, and back again. The
dark eyes returned to her face with an unmistakable
gleam of appreciation, and he said, 'Morris neglected
to say how beautiful you are.'

She stared, and gasped, and then stated the obvious
—unbelievable, but obvious. 'You can see!'

'You didn't know?'

'No.' She shook her head.

'I had an operation two years ago.' He looked at her
curiously, and she thought, *he doesn't know me*. There
must have been dozens of women in those years since
she had met him. He had never seen her, and obviously
her name had meant nothing when they were introduced. He probably thought it strange that someone
whose job was in the entertainment world should have
missed the news that one of its best-known stars had
regained his sight. He didn't know how completely she
had managed the difficult task of practically erasing
all knowledge of him from her life.

Morris came back and handed her a gin and tonic,
waiting for her confirmation that it was just as she
liked it, before giving Cade a glass of whisky and having one himself.

'Now for arrangements,' he said. 'Carrie, I want you
to arrange for a hire car, to be delivered here tonight.
Do it by phone so you can't be followed. You'll do the
driving—you can start as soon as it gets dark. Take it
slowly, there's some tricky driving in the gorges.'

'I know,' Carissa murmured, appalled at the thought
of trying to negotiate some of those roads in the dark.

'*Very* slowly,' Morris repeated. 'You'll be followed from the time you leave here—by your bodyguards. They'll be with you all the way, so don't worry.'

Slightly reassured, Carissa sipped at her drink.

'Where are the bodyguards now?' she asked. 'Around —outside?'

'Yes. I saw one of them as we came in,' Morris told her.

'I'll need clothes,' she said.

'You can go and get some packing done later. Will you take long?'

'About half an hour. I don't suppose I'll need much for a fortnight in the wilds. I'd like to go back to the office, though. If I'm to be away for a while, there are things to be done.'

'That's probably a good idea. Would look less suspicious, wouldn't it?'

'Look, *do* you think you were followed from Australia?' Carissa asked.

'No. But we can't afford risks—just in case.'

Cade took little part in the discussion, sipping his whisky and slipping his glasses back on so that it was difficult to guess what he thought about it all. He looked, if anything, faintly bored by the whole affair.

Carissa was glad to be back in the office, though it was hard work getting everything sorted and ready for someone else to take over tomorrow. She left the office at the usual time and went to her flat, which she shared with another girl who worked at the city library. Cathy was used to having her flatmate go away for a few days, and wasn't too surprised at the suddenness of this trip and the uncertain duration.

By nine-thirty they were on their way, the comforting headlights of the green Mercedes that Morris had discreetly pointed out as their escort, shining in the rear vision mirror of their hired Zephyr as Carissa competently pulled out into the street and headed for the southern motorway.

She concentrated on her driving, trying her best to ignore the man beside her, as she trod on the accelerator and held it at the maximum of the speed limit, glancing in the rear vision mirror to ensure their shadow was still with them.

She saw Cade glance over his shoulder and felt the quick scrutiny he gave her before returning his eyes to the wide ribbon of road in their headlights. Consciously she tried to relax, reminding herself that so far as he was concerned he had never seen her in his life before today. Certainly she had no intention of reminding him of that other disastrous meeting. Her own tingling awareness of him, his strong profile, his shoulder almost touching her, his long legs stretched out before him as he folded his arms and settled comfortably back in the seat, was a hangover from an experience that had been traumatic at the time, but was done with years ago. Certainly he had shown no particular consciousness of her, except the natural casual interest of an experienced man sizing up a pretty woman.

All the same, she wished she was certain that Morris had made it clear to Cade just what duties she was expected to perform for him. Morris had a way of sliding out of any direct confrontation with embarrassment or unpleasantness, and she wasn't sure if her hurried whisper to 'make it clear to him that my "wifely duties" stop at cooking and cleaning, you hear?' had been taken to heart.

'You're a good driver,' he said. His voice was quiet, but it startled her into tightening her grasp on the wheel. 'Do you mind being talked to while you drive?'

'No, not at all,' she answered coolly enough. Normally she would have felt grateful for the company to keep her alert. Now she was on tenterhooks, afraid of giving herself away, but he was a client and her job was to keep him happy. If he wanted to talk she had better let him. With luck she could keep her replies to noncommittal commonplaces.

'How far are we going?' he asked.

'A few hundred miles. It takes about five hours. We'll be there about two in the morning.'

'I *can* count.'

He didn't sound annoyed, just faintly mocking, but she said, 'Sorry.'

His head moved sharply as he looked at her, making her nerves jump. What had she said to startle him, for heaven's sake?

Casting about for something neutral to say, she asked, 'Do you drive?'

There was a momentary silence before he said, 'Yes. It was one of the first things I learned after the operation on my eyes. Would you like me to do some of the driving tonight? I'm not used to your left-hand road rules, but——'

'It's all right,' she said. 'Morris told me to do the driving.'

Again there was a small pause before he spoke, his voice mild but with a faint edge she couldn't quite analyse. 'You always do what Morris wants?'

'Mostly,' she said. 'He's my boss.'

She thought he was looking at her again, but kept her own eyes steadily on the road. In the darkness he couldn't see much, anyway, whatever he was looking for.

He asked, 'How long have you been working for him?'

'Five years.'

'As his personal assistant?'

'I started as a receptionist.'

'And worked your way up. Clever girl.'

She didn't quite like the way he said that, but there was nothing in the words she could take exception to. She pressed her foot down a little harder on the accelerator as they came out of a curve, and said nothing.

Cade lapsed into silence, too, but in spite of his relaxed pose she thought she could feel a faint tension emanating from him.

The headlights leaped ahead of them into the darkness. Traffic was lighter now, and flicking a glance in the mirror she thought she could see the lights of the Mercedes, that had been dropping back before.

Cade must have had a similar thought. He stirred and looked back again briefly, saying softly, 'They're still with us. I suppose Morris did fill you in on what this is all about?'

'He said your life had been threatened and you were supposed to hide out until the police could catch whoever is responsible.'

He made a restless movement, and she had an idea that he hadn't liked the word 'hide'. 'They know who's responsible,' he said. 'It's a matter of proof, of connecting the criminal with the—crime.'

'I see.'

'You're very calm,' he commented.

'It isn't me that's being threatened,' she reminded him.

He laughed softly, then, and at the remembered sound, so seemingly intimate in the closed, dark space of the car, she almost caught her breath, as painful memory flooded her being.

'You're with me,' he said. 'That places you in jeopardy to some extent, surely. For as long as we're together.'

'I gather there isn't really much danger,' she said. 'Morris was pretty sure you hadn't been spotted leaving Sydney. So whoever he is, he probably has no idea where you are by now. The guards are just insurance.

You'll be able to enjoy a few days at the lodge and
when the police have their evidence you can——'

'Come out of hiding?' he supplied a little sarcastically. 'Are you reassuring me, by any chance?'

'It's part of my job, Mr—Franklin,' with the faintest
trace of mockery.

'Tell me about the other parts,' he invited, with de-
ceptive mildness.

'Well, I'll show you about the place—the lodge has
extensive grounds, and there are beautiful bush walks
in every direction. And a boat, if you want to go on
the lake. I'll see to your meals, look after the lodge,
and—generally make you comfortable.'

'Comfortable? It sounds delightful.' She tried to
ignore the inflection in his voice, but he went on to
say, 'Haven't you missed out something?'

'What do you mean?'

'I gather this rather melodramatic plan of Morris's
involves a little play-acting. You, I understand, are
supposed to be my very new bride?'

Crisply she replied, 'If anyone asks, yes. It shouldn't
involve much play-acting. The lodge is quite secluded,
and there aren't a great many neighbours.'

'Now you sound exactly as Morris described you.'

'Do I?'

He waited, and when she didn't continue, he
laughed. 'You won't ask, will you? He said you were
competent and levelheaded and completely trustworthy. Unlikely to lose your head in any circumstances. He made you sound quite formidable. That's
why I was surprised when I saw you.'

'Were you? I wouldn't have known.'

'Wouldn't you? You were rather surprised yourself,
weren't you?'

'Yes,' she admitted, adding quickly, 'I hadn't known
about the operation to cure your blindness. I'm afraid
—I must have missed that bit of news.'

'You don't follow my career, then? Morris knew. I gathered the story had been fairly widely published here.'

'I've always admired your work,' she said.

'You're being tactful,' he mocked. 'No wonder Morris finds you the perfect assistant. Except'—unexpectedly he reached out and took her left hand from the wheel, running his thumb over her fingers—'you forgot to buy yourself a wedding ring.'

The contact sent a physical shock coursing through her, and she snatched her hand away from his.

'You shouldn't have done that,' she said to cover the action. 'I'm driving.'

The road was perfectly straight just now, and he glanced through the windscreen and then turned his head to look at her face. 'You think it's dangerous?' he asked. 'Here?'

'You took me by surprise,' she explained.

'I beg your pardon. Next time I'll give you fair warning.' His voice was amused, and she wondered if he guessed at the real reason behind her sudden naïve withdrawal. She should have shrugged and laughed, and casually taken her hand away.

'I don't think anyone thought of a ring,' she said. 'But it shouldn't matter. No one should be close enough to notice, anyway.'

'How soothing you sound, Carissa.' He leaned into the corner, watching her. 'So calm and confident. One would think you do this kind of thing every day.'

'Not quite this kind of thing,' she said. 'To tell the truth, it doesn't seem quite real—death threats and bodyguards aren't part of our scene, in New Zealand. At least, that sort of thing is pretty rare.'

'Do you always tell the truth, Carissa?' he asked softly.

His using her name made her feel uneasy. She didn't particularly like Morris's nickname, but she said hastily, 'Morris calls me Carrie, Mr—Franklin.'

'I like Carissa better, my pretend-bride. And don't you think it's a trifle old-fashioned to address your new husband as "Mr-er-Franklin"? Try "Cade".'

'Yes, of course.' He seemed to be waiting, but she didn't try it. Instead she asked, 'Would you like the radio on?'

Indifferently, he said, 'If *you* would. You're driving.'

She found the switches and put it on, and music flowed into the spaces in the conversation, which got longer as they drove on.

Once they left the motorway behind the road became more winding in parts, and she travelled more slowly. When, after three hours, she turned off the main road, she slowed to be sure their escort was still there, and as she saw the car turn picked up speed again. After a mile or so, though, the headlights behind them began to blink off and on, and she pulled in to the side of the road.

'What is it?' She had thought Cade was dozing, but he was wide awake now.

'I think they want us to stop,' she said, about to turn off the engine key.

He stopped her with a hand on her wrist. 'Leave it running.'

As a shape emerged from the car behind them and began coming towards their car, he took a torch from the glove box and leaned over to snick down the lock on her door, staying there, half across her as he switched on the torch and lowered the window.

The man caught in the beam blinked but didn't raise his hand to shield his eyes, and Cade switched off the beam.

'It's okay, Mr Franklin,' the man said quietly. Then, to Carissa he added, 'Would you switch off your lights, please, Miss Martin, and wait until we signal you to go on. We just want to check in case we're being followed.'

She did as he asked, and he disappeared back into the darkness.

'Switch off,' said Cade, and leaned back into his own seat.

Her fingers fumbled for the key and the throbbing of the engine died, to be replaced in her ears by the hurried beat of her heart. She told herself it was nerves— the dark night, the fantastic possibility that they could have been followed by a man bent on murder, the realisation that this secret drive through the night, those two men who were Cade's bodyguard, were part of real life, not elements in some fictional drama.

But it wasn't that. The reason for that heightened awareness was the man who now sat silent beside her. The reason was that he had touched her, his shoulder pressing against hers, his coat brushing against her breast as he leaned across the car. She had been conscious of his warmth, the faint aroma of soap and aftershave, his cheek so close she could have kissed it.

And what disturbed her more than anything was the almost overwhelming desire she had experienced to do so—to do so and have him turn his head in the darkness after the other man had gone and find her mouth with his.

CHAPTER THREE

THEY sat on in the dark silence, Cade with his head half-turned over his shoulder, sitting sideways so that he could watch behind them. Carissa looked straight ahead into the blackness, carefully making each breath controlled and even while sounds filtered into the car from the night outside. The soft rustle of leaves as a night breeze stirred the thick growth of native trees lining the road, the sleepy thrum of a single cricket, the distant call of a morepork on the watch for some unwary prey. The muted hum of a car's engine on the main road that they had left came closer and then faded into the distance again without faltering, and Cade moved slightly as he relaxed. Once more the same sound from the same direction, and then silence.

After fifteen minutes headlights blinked on behind them, and Cade touched her shoulder briefly and said, 'Let's go.'

She had to drive more slowly now because the road became narrower and the hard tarseal gave way to gravel-topped clay. It was impassable sometimes in the winter when the rains brought slips down across it or washed part of it into one of the steep gullies. Green and yellow opossum eyes gleamed at them from the dark roadside and once a morepork flew across the bonnet, startling her into touching the brake briefly before she realised what the grey ghostly apparition was. Small insects fluttered into the beam of light ahead of them, and a moth hit the windscreen, briefly floundered and died.

Her eyes began to ache with strain and her head throbbed gently in sympathy. Cade had switched off the radio when they stopped, and she said, 'Do you mind if we have the radio on again?'

He reached out and put it on and asked, 'Are you all right?'

'Yes, I'm fine,' she said with false firmness. 'Just getting a bit bored. It's a long drive, in the dark.'

He said, 'Is that a reflection on my company? Would you like me to talk to you?'

'Of course not,' she said.

'Of course not—*what*?'

'It isn't a reflection on your company,' she explained. 'I said it was the drive that was boring, not you. Talk if you like, but I don't expect you to keep me entertained.'

The other way round, in fact, she thought. At least, Morris expected her to keep Cade entertained for a few days or more. If she had known who it was before she agreed to take on the job wild horses couldn't have made her do it. But once she had done so there was no way she could think of to back out without making Morris suspicious. And even then, she hadn't any inkling what this man could do to her with the merest, most casual touch. She had to keep remembering she was now a mature twenty-five, not an idiotic seventeen. No way was she going to repeat the greatest blunder of her life.

Cade didn't talk much, but he did ask a few questions about the country they were passing through, even though he couldn't see it in the dark. Carissa told him they were not far from Rotorua, New Zealand's famous tourist resort where volcanic activity included boiling pools of mud and water, and the famous geysers shooting scalding hot water into the air. There were odd pockets of thermal activity in this area, too, and one of the attractions of the lake was a nearby swimming pool of natural hot water fed by a spring. The lake itself lay in a basin almost entirely surrounded by native bush which grew down to the water's edge, except in a few places where a narrow strip of sand sloped into the water, ideal for swimming and boating.

'The lodge has its own private foreshore,' she said. 'And a small freshwater inlet. Are you a fisherman?'

'No. I've tried it once or twice, but I'm not dedicated to the sport.'

'There are trout in the lake, and in the streams that feed it. Morris likes to fish here. You probably saw his prize fish in his apartment.'

'In the bedroom, yes. I thought the usual place for such trophies was a prominent place in the living room.'

'Oh, Morris is modest in his way. And he says it cheers him to wake up to the sight of an eight-pound rainbow trout.'

She felt the sideways glance he flicked at her as he murmured, 'I can think of nicer things to wake up to.'

She was glad he couldn't see her expression. She would have to school herself not to show her emotions to him. Well, Morris said she was a cool ice-maiden, an opinion apparently shared by the few men she had allowed to enter her life for a time. If she could fool them she could fool Cade too. Not that she had needed to try very hard, before. There had never been very much danger of her letting any of them go half as far as Cade had. She had learned a bitter lesson when she was seventeen, and learned it well.

'Are you dedicated to any sport?' she asked coolly, leading away from the subject.

'Not as a player,' he said. 'I have done some karate and judo, and I swim. I followed baseball for many years, though. Seeing my first game after the operation was something—well, *something*.'

Carissa swallowed on an unexpected ache in her throat and steadied her voice with deliberation. 'It isn't played very much here. Tell me about it.'

He told her, and she listened and asked questions she hoped sounded intelligent, intoxicated by the beautiful voice she remembered so well, so that it didn't matter what he talked about, so long as she could keep on listening to it.

She stopped at the iron gate to the lodge and fumbled in her bag for the key to the padlock on it. The Mercedes drew up behind them as she got out of the car, and the man got out again and came over to her. She pointed out the side track that led to the fishermen's hut, and he told his partner to drive down there. 'If you don't mind, I'll come with you,' he said.

He took the key and opened the gate for her, then climbed into the back of the car after she drove through and he had locked it again.

When she drew up outside the garage behind the house, he said, 'Just stay here, please. I'll look round first.'

She felt Cade move restlessly beside her as the man opened the garage door and went in, a torch beam bobbing about as he shone it around. Then he came out and told her, 'Okay, so far. Can I have the house keys, please.' She gave them to him and he said, 'Stay in the car until I come back. Don't move yet.'

Cade moved restlessly and then impatiently opened the door.

'He said to stay here,' Carissa reminded him.

'*He* works for *me*,' said Cade. '*I* give the orders.'

She wasn't sure who actually had hired the two men —she understood it was Morris, but no doubt Cade would ultimately foot the bill. 'He's doing his job,' she protested. 'Why not let him get on with it?'

He muttered something under his breath, still holding the door slightly open, and she knew he wanted to go and join the other man, not cower in a car.

'Besides,' she added, remembering she had been detailed to look after him, too, but not expecting that argument to carry any weight at all, 'I don't fancy being left on my own here.'

He looked at her sharply and shut the door with a snap. 'You're nervous?' he asked. 'I thought you were the original cucumber lady.'

'Well, I'm not,' she said somewhat shortly, because she didn't fancy herself as the Little Woman who screamed and fainted at the first smell of danger. She wouldn't admit to herself that what she had said was the simple truth, but she had to let him think so. Only there was no need to make a production of it.

Unexpectedly she felt his cool fingers on her wrist, and he drawled with sardonic amusement, 'I do believe your pulse rate is a little fast, at that.'

Carissa wasn't surprised. It must be jumping all over the place, with the memories he was unknowingly invoking. She suddenly hated him, for arousing her this way without even trying, for being who he was, and what he was, with his careless charm that altered a girl's life and left her unfit for any other man while he *didn't even remember*, let alone cherish what they had shared, once. Most of all she hated him for not remembering.

This time she didn't snatch her hand away from his touch, though she had an urgent and primitive desire to do it, and hit out at him in a fury of pain and anger. She pulled away without haste but firmly, and he let her go.

The bodyguard came back, with his mate, and when she asked, 'How did *he* get in?' the first one chuckled and said,

'Mr Wyatt gave us a spare gate key. He used it after he put our car out of sight. It's all clear, and I switched on the generator for you. Our number is on your telephone pad. Goodnight.'

Cade said, 'Thanks, Stan. Goodnight. Goodnight, Pat.'

'Stan? Pat?' Carissa queried as she drove into the

garage. 'When were you introduced?'

'While you were at the office, of course. They could hardly do the job without all of us having a good look at each other, could they?'

She supposed not. 'I'm not used to this cloak and dagger stuff,' she muttered, opening her door.

'Neither am I,' she heard him say as they both got out. But looking at him in the faint glow from the interior light of the car, she thought he looked big and dark and dangerous, and that he didn't mind too much about the danger. She wondered if he would regard it as one of the new challenges presented to him by the operation that had restored his sight.

They carried their luggage into the small kitchen, and she said, 'I'll just put on the kettle and show you a room. There are plenty to choose from.'

She filled the kettle and plugged it in, then led him upstairs, leaving her own case and overnight bag in the kitchen.

She opened the door of the first room upstairs and said, 'Will this be all right? It has a shower and toilet through there.' She nodded towards the door at one side of the room.

'It looks fine.' He put his case and his guitar on the blue-quilted bed, and she went out to the hall cupboard and scooped out some sheets and towels. She brought them back into the room and said, 'I'll make up the bed later,' and went into the small bathroom to place the towels on the rail there and unwrap the new cake of soap in the cupboard over the small hand-basin. She screwed up the stiff paper into a ball and holding it in her hand, walked into the bedroom again. Cade had taken off his jacket and tie and undone some of the buttons of his shirt. He looked very masculine like that, a narrow vee of tanned skin showing between the edges of his shirt. Masculine and wildly handsome. His good looks were even more devastating now that his dark eyes were no longer hidden by glasses.

Carissa said, 'Coffee will be ready in about five minutes. Unless you prefer something else.'

His mouth quirked into a faintly sardonic smile but he said, 'Coffee sounds fine, thank you.'

He came down with her and as she switched off the jug which was burbling happily on the bench, he asked, 'Where do you want these?' and picked up her luggage.

'I'll take them up later,' she told him.

He didn't put them down, merely said again, 'Where do you want them?'

She hadn't thought about it, and when he asked, 'Will the room next to mine do?' she said 'Yes. Thank you,' almost too hastily, because it threw her into a near panic and that was too stupid for words. What difference did it make? They were alone in the house anyway and whether she slept next door to him or at the far end of the not very long passageway, what did it matter, really?

He returned just as she put two steaming cups on the table, and placed a sugar bowl between them. 'Cream?' she asked, holding a small tin.

'No, thanks. Black.'

She had known, but congratulated herself on pretending not to. 'There's plenty of food here,' she said, 'but milk and eggs have to come from the store further round the lake. I'll get some in tomorrow.'

They drank their coffee in silence, and she picked up the empty cups to wash them, almost falling as she stumbled over the leg of her chair on getting up.

Cade was on his feet, steadying her, his arm on her waist and a hand firm on her elbow.

'Thank you,' she said. She moved out of his hold, but he took the cups from her and said, 'I'll wash them. You're beat. Go to bed.'

Too tired to argue, Carissa went upstairs, but there was *his* bed to make, first. She had put the sheets on and was smoothing the blankets over them when he walked into the room.

'I told you to go to bed,' he said, sounding irritated. 'And I meant yours, not mine. Unless you're planning to share that with me?'

If she hadn't been so tired she would have kept her temper—and her head. As it was she snapped the first thing that came into her mind. 'I'm only doing my job, Mr—Franklin. And that's *all* I'm going to do. You may find it difficult to believe, but I've no desire to share any bed with you *ever*——' *again*, she had almost said. Appalled, she stopped herself just in time. 'I'm sorry,' she said, looking at his face, that had gone hard and cruel, the eyes narrowed and glittering and the mouth unmistakably grim. 'I'm sorry, I shouldn't have said that, I'm very tired.'

'Yes, you are,' he agreed, those merciless eyes on her pale face, the faint blue shadows about her darkened eyes. 'If it wasn't for that I'd be very tempted to make you take that back.'

Her heart bumped with fear and the room seemed to execute a gentle swaying action before righting itself again. She closed her eyes momentarily and realised that her headache was worse. With a faint shake of her head she opened them again.

Cade still looked grim, but his voice was almost gentle as he said, 'Now, get out of here, before I change my mind.'

When she woke it seemed very bright. She had a vague memory of drawing the curtains before she had climbed into bed last night, a hastily made bed that had nevertheless looked immensely inviting after the fraught day she had been through. Her head had been throbbing in earnest by then, and she had taken two aspirins in the bathroom after cleaning her teeth. Thank goodness the ache seemed to have gone.

She opened her eyes and found a large shadow blocking the window. Cade.

'I brought you some breakfast in bed,' he said pleasantly, and she saw the tray with a plate of bacon and buttered toast on her bedside table, and a cup of tea.

'No eggs, I'm afraid,' he told her. 'But there's plenty of frozen bread and butter.'

'You shouldn't have,' she said. 'But thank you.' She sat up, pulling up a flimsy strap that fell from her shoulder. 'What's the time?'

'Ten o'clock. You were dead to the world at eight, but I looked in again twenty minutes ago and you seemed to be stirring.'

She tried to take the tray, and he crossed the room and said, 'Let me.'

He settled the tray across her and sat on the bed. Carissa ate a little selfconsciously, wishing he would go away, but he talked about the view from the house across the lake and the trophies adorning the walls downstairs.

'Did Morris bag the stag, too?' he asked, referring to the head of a magnificent twelve-pointer that took pride of place in the large dining room.

'No, Morris is no hunter. It belonged to the previous owner. The house was put up for sale when he died. A lot of the furnishings came with it. I hate that thing, myself, it puts me off my food. But some of the guests find it impressive, and it's a talking point, so Morris left it there.'

'I don't see much sport in shooting a deer, myself. Skill, I suppose, but if I was a hunter I think I'd prefer something that at least could fight back.'

Yes, you would, she thought. *I can see you going after tigers.* Aloud she said. 'We're short on dangerous animals in New Zealand. I believe wild pigs can get pretty fierce, though. Tuskers have been known to kill dogs, and turn on hunters.'

'You've just persuaded me to take up fishing,' he said lazily.

Carissa laughed, which was probably what he wanted. She didn't believe him, of course. He wasn't the type to be put off by danger. More likely it would stimulate him. He must have hated being blind.

But he smiled back at her, and she hastily lifted her teacup and drained it so that she needn't look at him. When he smiled he was too attractive altogether.

He took the empty tray from her, but instead of getting up and taking it away with him, he placed it back on the table, then turned to put his hands on either side of her on the bed, trapping her against the pillows.

Still faintly smiling, he said, 'You look just like a new bride. I rather fancy being a honeymoon husband, waking up to you in the morning, Carissa.'

'Well, you're not,' she retorted, trying to sound light-hearted but firm. 'And there's no need to pretend. No one can see us.'

His smile broadened a little, and she wondered if that remark had been a mistake. 'What about a little practice?' he said. 'Good morning, darling.' And he leaned forward and kissed her.

His mouth was firm and warm, but as kisses go it was fairly innocuous and nothing to get excited about. If she hadn't panicked and tried to shove him away with her hands on his shoulders, he would probably have left it at that.

But she had guessed right about him, and opposition was a challenge, obviously. She found her wrists firmly held as he pressed her head back against the pillow and his mouth became dangerously exciting on hers, persistent, seeking and determined. Her resistance was hopelessly inadequate from the start, with her legs trapped by the blankets, Cade's hard chest imprisoning her body and inflexible against the softness of her breasts, and his hands keeping her wrists helplessly pinned to the bed.

She made herself stop fighting because it wasn't going to get her anywhere, but the sweet punishment had only begun. When he felt her taut muscles relax, his body seemed to settle closer to hers, and though he lifted his mouth it was only to kiss her throat and shoulder and then move warmly to the curve of her breast.

She protested then with a feeble shake of her head, saying, 'No—don't!' And while her lips were still parted on the word he covered them again with his in a silent, seeking, devastating demand until she capitulated and gave him the response he wanted. She was swept into a vortex of dizzying delight, and when he released one of her wrists and slid his hand warmly on to the soft swell of her breast, she didn't protest, only moved her hand to touch his hair gently with her fingers as he went on kissing her.

When he finally paused again and moved away from her, she lay bemused and quiescent while he surveyed her flushed face, a hint of a smile tugging the corners of his mouth.

'Now,' he said softly, 'what was that you were saying last night, Miss Martin?'

She felt as if the breath had stopped in her throat. She could only lie there and watch as he picked up the tray and moved towards the door. He was nearly there when she found voice enough to say, 'One swallow doesn't make a summer, Mr Franklin.'

He didn't answer, just stopping in the doorway to look back at her, but the look was merciless, flickering over her like a burning finger. In his eyes she saw how she looked, with her pale hair spread on the pillow, her cheeks still flushed, her lips still throbbing from his kisses, and the strap of the nightgown had fallen again—(or had he pushed it aside?) exposing her bare shoulder and the beginning curve of her breast.

Involuntarily she put up a hand to straighten it, and then wished she hadn't, when she saw the amused smile he watched her with, before he turned away.

She would go away. Getting out of bed, gathering up clothes to put on, using the bathroom and brushing her hair, Carissa kept that one thought in mind. She could not possibly stay here with *him*, not for another day. He had his two bodyguards. Her presence was totally unnecessary, just an extra frill that could well be done without. She would go back to Auckland and tell Morris ...

Tell Morris what?

That she quit—that from here on Cade Franklin or Cadiz Fernand could look after himself? *Why?* Morris was going to ask. She would tell him she was scared— but she had accepted the assignment far too readily and phlegmatically for him to accept that she was suddenly overwhelmed with fear for her safety now. Besides, her pride revolted at the idea of letting Morris think she was a coward.

Tell him that Cade had made a pass? He would think she was crazy. Fending off passes was all in a day's work, as well he knew, and she had never had any difficulty before in doing it with finesse and tact—it was one of the reasons Morris employed her for just this sort of thing, looking after his show business personalities off-stage.

If she said Cade had tried to force her—but reluctantly she admitted there was no justice in that. Certainly she hadn't been a willing party, at first, and he had held her down, but she had been in no danger of rape. Another danger, perhaps, that arose from within herself, but she had no grounds for a serious accusation against him, and it would be a despicable thing to do. She couldn't leave, there was no plausible excuse.

By the time she had got dressed and made the bed and hung up the remainder of her clothes in the roomy wardrobe, she was left with no alternative but to go downstairs, unless she was to spend the day skulking in her room, which seemed both childish and weak-minded. And she had come to the reluctant conclusion that she had to stay and see this thing through. She could only hope that Cade's would-be assassin would soon be caught.

If she played it decidedly cool from now on she would be in no danger, she decided. She had flicked Cade's masculine pride last night and she had to admit, trying to be philosophical about it, that he had certainly proved a point this morning. She tried to thrust down a burning anger born of humiliation, and tell herself that if she presented no further provocation he would be unlikely to try to repeat the performance. For all he knew, after all, they were practically total strangers, having only met yesterday.

He wasn't in the house. His bed had been neatly made, she discovered when she tapped on his door and peeped in to see if she should attend to that, and the kitchen was clean and tidy with not a dish in sight.

She went out and found him standing with his back to her near the lake's edge, across the wide lawn. Suppressing an impulse to turn and go back inside, she strolled across to join him.

Long before most people would have noticed her presence, he had turned to watch her coming towards him. He still had his blind person's facility for using every sense to its highest degree.

As she stopped a few feet from him he said, 'Don't you think a loving bride would come closer and take my arm? There are witnesses.'

There were a couple of boats on the lake, fishermen trying their luck.

'They're more interested in the fish than in us,' she said. But she tucked her hand into his arm with what she hoped was a casual air, bringing an amused glint to his eyes which stirred her to faint anger again.

'Satisfied?' she asked.

Cade looked down at her and his eyes gleamed as he said, 'Hardly,' then laughed when her cheeks warmed with colour.

She threw him a look of pure hatred that at least made him stop laughing as his brows rose questioningly. He stopped her attempt to withdraw her hand by clamping hard fingers over it on his arm. 'Spoiling for a fight, aren't you?' he teased callously. 'You wouldn't win.'

'Physical strength isn't everything,' she flashed at him.

'Agreed.' His eyes roved over her. 'You have weapons of your own. But they'd be more effective if you didn't show so plainly that you don't like me.'

'I don't dislike you,' she said stiffly, remembering she had a job to do. Then, resentment overwhelming her sense of duty, she added, 'You can't blame me for being angry—you deliberately humiliated me!'

He looked down at her and asked, 'By kissing you— or by not carrying things further than kisses? Were you disappointed?'

Furious, she managed to wrench her hand at last from his grasp. 'You have an outsize ego!' she snapped. 'Of course I wasn't *disappointed*! I'd much prefer that you didn't touch me at all.'

'That might be a little difficult,' he drawled, looking faintly amused. 'We're supposed to be a loving couple.' Abruptly, he said, 'Come for a walk along the shore. Our guardian angels next door are about, they'll be able to watch us.' He turned her along the pale sand near the water.

'It's as beautiful as you said,' Cade told her, his eyes narrowed slightly against the shimmer of the sun on the lake's dappled surface.

Forgetting her vendetta for a moment, she said, 'It must be marvellous for you——'

'Being able to see again? Yes, it is,' he said quite soberly. 'I don't think I'll ever be able to take it for granted as so many people do.'

'You'd been blind since you were nineteen, hadn't you?' she asked.

'Yes.' He changed the subject, pointing to one of the trees growing almost at the water's edge and asking her if she knew what it was. She looked at the dark red velvet trumpets of flowers surrounded by sharp-toothed leaves and told him it was a rewarewa, or New Zealand honeysuckle tree. Happy to find a neutral subject to talk about, she discoursed on some of the other inhabitants of the bush, the tall kahikatea with its feathery leaves and purple-and-red fruits, the scarlet-flowering rata and the golden kowhai, prettiest of the forests' flowering trees.

'You're very knowledgeable,' he commented as they stopped where the lake intruded into the grounds of the lodge in a long narrow inlet.

'Not really. Morris's visitors are often interested in the trees and the wild life, so I've studied them up a bit since I've been bringing people to the lodge. There are several books back at the house, if you're really interested.'

He didn't answer at once, and she looked up at him enquiringly, to find him apparently studying her with some intentness.

At last he said softly, 'Oh, I'm interested,' but she didn't think he meant the trees. His eyes held hers deliberately with a masculine light of challenge, and it was an effort to keep her face politely blank and pull her gaze from his.

'We'd better go back,' she said as coolly as she could manage, and began to retrace their steps along the sand.

What on earth, she wondered, had she let herself in for? *Morris, damn you! You don't know what you've done.*

She vetoed Cade's company when she went to the shop later in the car. She would have liked to walk the mile and a half, but she was supposed to stick fairly closely to the house and Cade.

She had been to the shop often enough in the past to be on mildly friendly terms with the woman behind the counter, although they had never exchanged names.

'Oh, it's you!' the woman said. 'At Kamahi lodge, are you?'

'Yes.' Carissa consulted a shopping list ostentatiously. 'Where do you keep the eggs now?' she asked.

'Over there, dear.' As she turned, the woman's voice continued, 'There hasn't been anyone at the lodge for quite a while. Have you got many guests this time?'

Last time the lodge had been used, there had been quite a party—a singing duo with their girl-friends and several hangers-on. Carissa hadn't enjoyed it, but the celebrities went home happy.

Turning back to the counter, she metaphorically breathed deeply and said, 'No, not this time. Just me and—and my husband.'

The door banged to behind Stan as he entered the shop, and gave them an impersonal nod. Evidently she wasn't supposed to know him.

'Oh—I didn't know you were married,' the woman remarked.

'I—wasn't before,' said Carissa, trying to sound casual, and thinking, *Lord! I hope I'm doing this right*. She reached into a chilled unit for some butter, and

said, 'I'll need some milk, too. And could you slice a
pound of bacon for me, please?'

The woman was looking pleased and knowing as
Carissa put the butter on the counter beside the eggs.
Then her face flickered as she followed the movements
of Carissa's hands. 'Oh! I see,' she said, and turned to
get the bacon.

Stan was behind her when she drew up at the gate,
riding a motor bike and with a rifle slung over his
shoulder. 'I've got a permit,' he said, as she eyed it.
'Like to see you both later—come over,' he added, and
she blinked and said, 'Oh, all right.'

But he had already kicked the engine into life and
roared on down the side road, leaving her alone.

She passed on the message to Cade over a late lunch,
and he said, 'Okay, let's take another walk this afternoon. In the other direction this time.'

When they strolled by the hut, Stan was fiddling with
a rod and line on the bank nearby, and Pat was in a
boat on the lake, looking very much as though he had
nothing on his mind but the possibility of trout for
dinner.

Stan gave them a casual wave, and Cade took
Carissa's arm and walked over to him.

'How's fishing?' he asked casually.

'Nothing biting,' said Stan, his fingers busy untangl-
ing a knot in the nylon line. 'But,' he looked up, and
Carissa realised that the blue eyes in his rather non-
descript face were remarkably shrewd and alert, 'we
hear fishy stories from the locals.' He glanced quickly
at Carissa and then back to Cade. 'They reckon there's
more strangers about than usual, this time of the year.
Some of them Americans, too. So we hear. Might be
nothing in it, of course.'

Cade's hand tightened on her arm until it hurt, and
Carissa made a small protesting movement. The hard
fingers relaxed, but Cade didn't look at her.

Stan said, 'If you two go for any long walks, don't forget to let us know. The bush can be risky, you know. By the way, the lady forgot her ring this morning. The woman in the shop noticed.'

'I don't have one,' said Carissa.

'Would've been better to get one,' Stan remarked, as he flexed his rod. 'Better not talk too long. Binoculars can see a long way.' He nodded to them casually as Cade took the hint and led Carissa away.

'Let's walk,' said Cade, and slipped an arm about her shoulders, as they walked on. His eyes scanned the shoreline, resting speculatively on the small holiday homes and fishermen's huts nestled among the trees.

The road petered out at the lake's edge, and a litter of large rocks and smaller rounded stones barred the way. On the other side of the natural barrier a temptingly broad strip of white-gold sand could be glimpsed.

Cade hardly hesitated. 'Come on,' he said, and leaped lightly on to a flat-topped outcrop of rock, turning to take her hand and pull her up after him.

Carissa needed little help, for she had always been sure-footed as a cat about rocks and trees, and they soon landed on the sand at the other side, Cade unnecessarily swinging her down into his arms on the last leap.

He held her as she made to move out of his hold, his hands firm on her waist. She stiffened as they moved to hold her closer to him.

'Don't fight me,' he said softly. 'We may be watched —and we're honeymooners, remember?'

She let her body relax against the hard warmth of his, but her lips closed firmly against him as he kissed her mouth. 'You're a lousy actress,' he muttered against it.

She moved her mouth aside and said, 'That's enough, Cade. You've convinced anyone who's watching. Now let me go.'

'Are you giving me orders?' he asked softly, his

breath warm on the skin of her cheek.

'I'm telling you to let me go!' she snapped, desperate at the closeness of him, the temptation of her body that wanted to mould itself against him, to give in to remembered passion.

She started to struggle, and he said '*Stop it*,' his arms tightening as he kissed her again, unmercifully finding her mouth and crushing it into some sort of submission, sweeping her into a dark country where nothing mattered but the hot waves of desire that assailed her body under the touch of his hands—except her panicky need to escape it, not to give in to the beating needs of her senses.

Driven by a desperate instinct for self-preservation, she opened her teeth and nipped sharply at his lower lip, and he gave a muffled exclamation and lifted his head, his eyes blazing with anger into hers.

'*You bitch!*' he muttered, and without warning pushed her down on the cool sand, in the shadow of the rocks, pinning her beneath him, his hands holding her by the shoulders, his mouth cruelly set, with a faint trickle of blood on the lower lip. 'Just *try* that again!' he said before his head came down and she tasted his blood on her own mouth as it punished hers again with hard, angry passion.

There was nothing to do but endure it, and close her eyes against the weakness of tears that threatened.

When it seemed the kiss was going to last for ever, Cade lifted his mouth and his body, and the sun blazed on to her closed eyelids. She felt as though a storm had just swept her up and then dropped her, exhausted and battered, on the lake shore. She opened her eyes and saw Cade sitting beside her, wiping the back of his hand across his mouth and looking at it broodingly. She raised her hand to her own mouth and tentatively touched her fingers to the throbbing outline of her lips.

He glanced at her and said, 'All right, I'm sorry if I was rough. But you asked for it.' For an apology, it sounded remarkably savage.

Carissa closed her eyes again, and next time she opened them he was lying beside her, with his arm thrown across his eyes. The afternoon sun was hot, and she seemed to be floating in a limbo where nothing mattered any more, anyway. She drifted into a doze for a few minutes, then roused herself with difficulty, remembering that it was risky to sleep in hot sun.

Cade still lay there in the same position as she eased herself up off the sand, quietly, and stood up. She had turned her back on him when his voice said, 'Where are you going?'

'Back to the lodge.'

He stood up without comment and was by her side as she clambered back over the rocks. But this time she kept ahead and he didn't offer to help her.

Stan and Pat were pottering with their rods by the water, and she wondered if they were really keen on fishing. If not, the pastime must be boring and uncomfortable for them.

Carissa busied herself for the remainder of the afternoon making over-much work for herself in the preparation of a meal for the evening, and Cade fetched his guitar and took it into the lounge, playing it and the piano alternately, and she gathered he was writing a new song.

The conversation over their dinner was politely conventional on the surface, and she ignored the hint of mockery in some of Cade's remarks, exerting herself considerably to treat him just like any other of Morris's guests.

Afterwards she refused his help with the dishes, and finding him in the lounge, holding his guitar across his knees but staring into space, she took a thriller from the bookcase in one corner and settled down to read.

For a thriller it seemed remarkably dull, but she ploughed on with determination into the second chapter before every nerve tensed as Cade rose and came over to her chair.

'Try this,' he said. She looked up and found him holding out a ring to her—a circle of gold with a band of platinum decoration. It looked vaguely familiar, and she recalled she had seen it on his hand—the little finger of his right hand. 'I should have thought of it before.'

She didn't want to wear a ring of his, but as she hesitated, he grabbed impatiently at her left hand and pushed it on to the third finger.

He didn't let go of her hand but stood looking down at the ring with a bitter twist to his mouth. 'My mother's wedding ring,' he said, with a harsh inflection. Then he laughed in a way that chilled her.

She pulled her hand from his grasp urgently, and made to remove the ring, saying, 'I can't wear this!'

He leaned down and clamped her wrists with his strong hands. 'Why not?'

'How can you ask that?' she said angrily. 'I'm not your wife—it's a farce for me to wear your mother's ring. And it's loose on me. Supposing I lost it?'

He shrugged and straightened. 'It wouldn't matter. The ring has no sentimental value for me whatsoever.'

CHAPTER FOUR

CARISSA wore the ring, hating it, and always nervous in case it slipped from her finger, until she wound some thread about it at one side and made it feel safer.

She got up early in the mornings and made breakfast for them both before Cade came down, and after three days they had established a sort of routine. They strolled in the extensive grounds or by the lake, or along the road a couple of times each day, and in the afternoons they swam together and sunbathed on the narrow private strip of sand in front of the lodge. Sometimes Cade put his arm about her shoulders or waist, and once or twice she had stiffly reciprocated, for the sake of appearances in case anyone was watching.

Their conversations were polite and almost formal, and although he called her Carissa with the caressive inflection that never failed to disturb her senses, she seldom used his name if she could help it.

And there was an undercurrent of tension in the air that had little to do with the threat of danger that was their reason for being here. It grew from their relationship and the fact that they were alone and together so much of the time. She tried to forget that dangerous interlude by the lake, and Cade never referred to it, but it lay between them inevitably like an explosive device that needed to be tiptoed round to prevent a disaster of some sort. She should have been grateful that Cade seemed to be trying as hard as she was to forget it, that he never touched her except when there might be witnesses, and had not attempted again to kiss her at all.

Stan and Pat reported there seemed to be nothing to worry about—the Americans they had mentioned

turned out to have been here before, and no one
seemed to be taking any particular interest in the lodge.
When Cade mentioned he thought he'd like a bush
walk, Pat said he'd be about, but go ahead, he doubted
there was any risk. It was pretty difficult to reach the
lodge or the bush behind it except from the road or the
lake, and the hut commanded a good view of both.
They should be perfectly safe.

Carissa showed Cade a map with the walking tracks
marked. One started by the lodge grounds and came
out at the main road, near the entrance to a public
walkway leading to the summit of one of the many
bush-covered peaks near the lake.

'How long would it take to go all the way?' Cade
asked.

'About three hours. We'd have to leave straight after
lunch, if you want to do that walk.'

'Can you manage it?'

'Of course. I've done it several times.'

'We'll let Pat and Stan know where we're going then.'

The two men met them on the road as they emerged
from the first narrow track after the first half hour.
They were dressed for tramping, and Stan forged ahead
of them while Pat lagged discreetly in the rear.

Caed said nothing, but Carissa sensed a frustration
and annoyance about him as they traversed the uneven
path, their footfalls deadened by the accumulated
leaves from the overhanging bush trees.

She heard a distinctive bird call and stopped, looking
about the trees nearby for the source.

Cade followed suit, and she said softly, 'Have you
seen a tui? There——' She pointed to the black shape
with its curved beak and white neck ruff, high on the
branch of a puriri, and they stood close together as its
muted flute-call echoed again through the bush, followed by a series of odd, throaty sounds and then the
two-note flute call again.

When the bird left his perch with a whirr of wings and disappeared among the moving green umbrella of leaves overhead, Carissa turned to move on, blundering unexpectedly into a low-hanging frond of a black-trunked punga fern, automatically recoiling as it touched her face.

Cade was behind her, and as she backed into his hard chest, his arm came round her waist, steadying her.

She said, 'Oh, sorry,' and tried to move out of his hold, but instead of releasing her, he turned her to face him and pulled her close as he kissed her, gently and without haste, and she responded as naturally as breathing, without thought of denial.

When he stopped abruptly and raised his head she was momentarily disorientated, the world still spinning about her head. Then he moved, frowning and muttering something forceful under his breath as he put several inches between them, and Stan appeared around a bend in the track.

There was no one else at the summit when they reached it but Pat, and the four of them rested there, admiring the views of bush and water and eating sandwiches washed down with coffee from the light packs that they carried.

Then the two men left Cade and Carissa and promised to reconnoitre the track on the way back.

Cade leaned back against a nearby tree trunk, draping an arm casually across raised knees. Carissa finished replacing the thermos in the pack and, conscious that he was watching her with lazy pleasure in his eyes, sat leaning on one hand with her feet drawn up beside her, trying to concentrate on the view.

A faint breeze lifted her hair and stirred the collar of the soft knit blouse she wore with her jeans. Bird calls and the soft stirrings of leaves in the wind were the only sounds, and the lake glittered peacefully in the distance. They sat in silent companionship, the tensions of the last few days melted away by sun and exercise and the apparent infinity of the quiet bush.

Then Cade said softly, 'Come here,' and her nerves tightened as she willed herself not to respond. That one kiss on the track had been crazy but sweet, and she couldn't bring herself to regret it. But she would be mad to invite a repetition. Cade was bored with his enforced inaction and hoping to while away some time with a little lovemaking—and in a few days he would walk out of her life again and forget her as completely as he had before.

'*Carissa?*' he insisted.

To ignore him would constitute another challenge to his masculinity. Reluctantly, she sighed faintly and stirred, starting to rise. 'We'd better go,' she said. 'The angels will be worried about you.'

He shot out a hand and captured her wrist, pulling her off balance against him, and held her so that she lay against his chest, his raised thigh against her back.

'*Don't!*' she protested.

He examined her face critically. 'You didn't say "don't" when I kissed you before,' he reminded her.

Trying to keep her voice even, she said, 'That was before.'

'A woman's privilege?'

'Yes. I changed my mind.'

'Perhaps I can change it again.'

She turned her face so that he couldn't reach her mouth, but he kissed her cheek and her throat and gently nibbled the lobe of her ear until she could stand the gentle torture no longer. With a great effort of will, she muttered between clenched teeth, '*Stop it, Cade!*'

'Why stop it?' he asked, his voice dark with desire. 'I don't want to stop it. And you——?' He suddenly moved his hand and captured her chin, bringing her to face him, and his eyes challenged hers, fully aware of the emotion he had aroused. 'Kiss me, Carissa,' he said, the words feathering her mouth. 'You want to. I can see it in your eyes.'

'No——' but even as she whispered the denial, her mouth parted under the demand of his, and he gathered her closer to him, then laid her down on the leaf-covered ground, one arm supporting her shoulders and head, and the other hand gently but insistently exploring the softness of her breast.

She couldn't think—she didn't want to think. She wanted only to give in to this blind tide of shivering ecstasy that was sweeping her away under the touch of his lips and his hands as they caressed, explored, insisted on knowing her in the age-old sense, on discovering the responses that her body could not help but make.

His mouth was against the base of her throat and he whispered a word—a phrase—in Spanish, waking long-denied memories of another time, another place. She didn't know what the words meant, only that they were love-words and that she had heard them before—when they had meant nothing.

As they meant nothing now.

Cade was leaning on his elbow, lifting himself away a little while he found the buttons of her blouse—and she rolled away from him suddenly and stood up, choking out her rejection. 'No! I don't *want* you, Cade. I can't——' And as he got to his feet and came for her, eyes glittering and his hand reaching for her, she almost screamed, 'No! Leave me alone!'

His breathing was audible, and his mouth suddenly cruel. 'Yes, you're very good at changing your mind, aren't you? But you're a liar, Carissa. You want me. You think I can't tell? Even a blind man knows when a woman wants him, if he knows anything about women at all.'

'And you know plenty!' she flashed. 'You've had so many women, haven't you?'

He looked suddenly wary. 'A few.'

She laughed derisively. 'That must be the under-statement of the year!'

Sharply he said, 'What's that supposed to mean?'

Carissa shrugged and turned away, wishing she had kept quiet.

His hands dragged her round again to face him, his dark eyes blazing into hers. 'Are you jealous because there've been other women in my life?'

Desperate to cover up, she said, 'Don't be ridiculous. It doesn't matter in the slightest to me what you do with your life or how many women you have. I'm just telling you that I won't be one of them, that's all.'

'Ten minutes ago I wouldn't have taken a bet on that.'

'You're an attractive man,' she admitted huskily. 'I got a little—a little carried away. I didn't mean it.'

'Is it Morris?' he asked.

'What?'

He dropped his hands from her shoulders and said, 'You're Morris's girl, aren't you? He should have told me straight out, instead of beating about the bush.'

Feeling her way, she said, 'Did he beat about the bush?'

'Some. I gathered I was being tactfully told it was hands off as far as you were concerned, but he didn't explain why. I only began to get the picture in the car on the way to the lodge.'

As noncommittally as possible, she said, 'I see.' She didn't see at all, but it seemed safer to pretend she did. She didn't remember saying anything which could have meant that she and Morris were more than boss and employee.

But if Cade thought they were, perhaps she should let him go on thinking it. It was probably the wisest thing to do. Only the thought didn't make her feel any better.

There was no sign of the angels on the road, but when they emerged from the last part of the track near the lake Stan was waiting for them. 'Everything's quiet here,' he said. 'Pat checked the road, and there's nothing to worry about.'

Cade thanked him and he went off in the direction of the road.

They let themselves into the house and Carissa went upstairs and treated herself to a hot shower and a change of clothing. She put on a light Indian cotton caftan with embroidered sleeves and neckline, and left her hair loose after brushing it until it gleamed. Then she went to the kitchen and cooked a couple of pieces of thick steak and made a salad, and an apple charlotte to be served with ice cream.

Cade came down as it was almost ready. He had showered too, and his hair was still faintly damp. He was wearing dark trousers and a close-fitting knit shirt in a cream colour that showed up his tanned skin and made him look achingly handsome.

Carissa was surprised at her own hunger when she sat down to eat, and Cade seemed to appreciate her cooking. He had opened a bottle of wine from Morris's cupboard, and it went well with the steak. Carissa thought it a good idea, helping to relax them both after the rather strained atmosphere that had prevailed since their ascent of the hill.

He insisted on helping her with the dishes, saying she must be tired after their long walk, but afterwards he suggested a short stroll along the lake. 'A gentle stroll,' he emphasised. 'Just along the sand.'

It was dusk, and she hesitated, but the house felt stuffy and hot, and a stroll in the fresh air would round the day off very nicely.

'All right,' she agreed. 'That sounds nice.'

The sand was cool in the evening, and there was no wind stirring the waves. The surface of the lake was still and smooth, glossed by the fading light of the sunset.

He took her hand in a firm clasp, and after an experimental attempt to tug it free, which he totally ignored, she let it stay there, gradually relaxing as he made no attempt to draw her closer to him.

'I enjoyed that walk,' he said. 'I don't do enough of that sort of thing.'

'You wouldn't have had much chance before——'

'Before I got my sight back—no. It wasn't nearly so much of a pleasure when I had to hang on to someone's arm all the time. And couldn't see what they saw.'

'It must have changed your life,' she said softly.

'Of course.'

'I'm sorry, that was an inane remark——'

'*Don't* keep saying you're sorry,' he said, stopping to grasp her shoulders in his hands. 'And it wasn't inane. It was true.'

She shivered a little at the touch of his hands, and he asked, 'Are you cold?'

'Not really.' She moved, and his hands dropped.

Walking on, she asked, 'Did you find the world very different, after the operation?'

'Some things, yes. I don't give live performances any more, you know—at least, not often.'

'Why not?'

'Because it isn't the same, now that I can see the audience. Before, I could sense them—*feel* them out there. But I couldn't see them. I find I preferred it when I couldn't see them.'

'Do they—make you nervous?'

He looked at her in the gathering darkness and said, 'No—it's something I can't describe. The magic is gone.' His gaze turned to the sky, where tiny points of light began to dance in the darkening haze. 'Well,' he shrugged, 'I'm concentrating more on recordings and composing now. That's one reason I could afford to come here for a while. No engagements in the offing for the next month or two.'

'You could have cancelled.'

'No. I would never have done that.'

She believed him. 'You must be glad—doubly so—that you're no longer blind, with this thing happening. You would have hated feeling vulnerable to an unseen enemy, wouldn't you?'

Cade glanced at her without saying anything, but she caught an odd, grim smile on his face, and said, 'You would really rather be out there fighting, wouldn't you, instead of staying here in relative safety?'

'Yes, I would. Does it show?'

'All the time. What happened in Melbourne? Morris said you were attacked.'

'They made a mistake. They sent a hit man with a knife. He ended up in hospital.'

'*They?*'

'A minor brotherhood.'

Shock held her rigid for a moment. 'You mean—like the *Mafia?*'

'In a small way, yes. I believe so.'

'But *why?* What had you done to them?'

'Nothing. There's a man who thinks he has a grudge against me. They wanted him in their organisation, and I think the price of having him was that they should eliminate me.'

'That's *incredible!*'

'It's guesswork, mainly. But I think it's what's happening.'

'Did you have bodyguards in Melbourne?' she asked.

'No. I didn't think they'd follow me there. The police back home were working on a hot lead, and I thought they'd have it sewn up by the time we finished in Australia.'

'Then how come the—the knife man ended up in hospital?'

Even in the darkness she could see the grim enjoyment of his smile. 'When I was fifteen I was running with a gang in New York. I've fought knives before, and old habits die hard. He thought I was an easy target. Over-confidence is the hit man's worst fault. I broke his jaw—among other things.'

Feeling slightly sick, she said shakily, 'You enjoyed it.'

He turned on her, his bulk almost menacing in the dark, and said roughly, 'No, I didn't *enjoy* it. But I'm damned glad I'm alive and he's out of action for a good long while—maybe he'll never wield a knife again. And I'm glad of *that*, too. Is that unnatural? Does it make me a monster?'

'No.' She almost whispered it, trying to see his face, his eyes. 'No, it doesn't. I'm so——'

She never finished the apology on her lips, because his hand suddenly came up under her chin and he tipped her head back and kissed her, hard.

He wasn't touching her in any other way, and it didn't occur to her to try and stop him. Not until he lifted his mouth from hers did she realise that her neck was aching.

His hand slipped to her shoulder and his other hand slid into her hair as he tipped her head again. 'The hell with Morris,' he said thickly, and kissed her again.

If she had been capable of speaking then, she might have echoed him. Not only Morris but the whole world seemed supremely unimportant compared with the intoxication of Cade's mouth on hers, his hands moulding her shoulders, then sliding down her back to press her closer to the urgency of his body, finding the feminine curves and hollows of hers.

His heart beat heavily against the palm of her right hand, and she slipped the left one up to his shoulder and then into his hair, letting him know that she wanted him to go on kissing her that way, parting her lips hungrily with his, making her answer his every sensuous demand.

He had gathered her so closely that her body was curved against him off balance, her toes barely touching the sand, and she felt him swing her slightly sideways as though he meant to lower her to the ground, when a sudden blinding beam of light struck them.

'What the hell——!' Cade muttered, and abruptly thrust her away, so that Carissa staggered before righting herself. He had started forward when the torch beam swung back to reveal Stan's face briefly before the man switched it off.

'Sorry, Mr Franklin, Just checking up,' he said.

'Oh, for God's sake!' Cade sounded thoroughly fed up.

'We saw you going out, and when it got dark and you weren't back, we thought we'd better make sure—— Well, I guess you're all right. Goodnight.'

His shadowy figure disappeared along the sand, and an empty silence fell behind him.

Cade was standing slightly away from her, as Carissa pushed her hair back behind her ears and tried to restore her feelings and her breath to normal. 'We'd better go in,' she said, as soon as she felt she could trust her voice.

Cade stretched his hand out to her like a challenge rather than an invitation, testing if she was still in the same mood.

She walked right past him, ignoring it. Ignoring, too, the sharp intake of his breath before he fell into step beside her.

They walked back in silence, but every nerve in her body was conscious of his presence—and the furious frustration of his mood. She felt frightened and excited and appalled at herself, all at the same time. She must have been mad. She *was* mad. He could make her crazy with a touch, forgetting the past, the future, the utter futility of thinking about any sort of lasting relationship with a man like Cade. She must *never* let him touch her again, never give in even for a moment to the temptation of his kisses. Her emotional equipment wouldn't stand for it.

The minute they got into the house she said hastily, 'I'm going to bed.'

'With me,' he stated flatly.

'No!' He had turned on the light, and his eyes were narrowed and dangerous. 'Not with you,' she said, stopping herself just in time from saying, *I'm sorry*. She should say it, because only ten minutes ago she had been clinging to him and letting him make love to her like a girl who was incapable of saying no. Which she had been, then. If ever a man was led on, she supposed he had been. So she certainly owed him some kind of apology, only for some reason he always reacted strongly to her apologies, and she was well aware that he was strung up and likely to do something fairly violent if she provoked him.

'No?' His question was soft but meaningful, and she battled down the nervous trembling that threatened to weaken her.

'That's what I said,' she stated bravely, her chin at a defiant angle.

'Would you have said it—out there?'

'I'm saying it now.' She hoped that sounded final, as she made to pass him and go up the stairs.

He hardly moved at all, but he was suddenly effectively blocking her way. 'Supposing I say otherwise?'

'You don't have the right.' She tried to sound calm and confident, sure of herself.

'Does Morris?' he asked harshly. 'If he wants rights, he should give you a ring. You're not wearing his ring.' He paused. 'You're wearing mine.'

After a moment's silence Carissa said, 'You know that means nothing. It's play-acting.'

'Were you play-acting out there?'

She looked away from him and said in a low voice, 'No.' Her eyes lifted and she said, 'You know I wasn't. But I don't want to follow it up. I'm not the type for a casual affair.'

His eyebrows rose a fraction and he smiled mockingly. 'What "type" is that? I never met a woman who would admit she was "that type". They all persuade themselves that theirs is a fashionably "meaningful" relationship. At least men tend to be more honest.'

'With themselves, perhaps. Not with women.'

'What does that mean?' he asked.

'That men make promises—and pretend love, to get what they want.'

His eyes were cool and steady. 'Did I promise you anything? Did I say I loved you?'

'No.'

'I want you. And don't pretend you don't feel the same. Isn't it enough?'

'Not for me.'

'You would rather have the lies?'

'I would rather have *nothing*! I don't want anything without love.'

He looked at her with a kind of weary cynicism. 'I don't know how to love,' he said. 'I never learned.'

Appalled, Carissa blinked. 'What sort of life have you had?'

'A good one,' he drawled, 'these last dozen years. My childhood was rough, but it was a good preparation for life in a jungle. And that's what my world is—a jungle. The survival of the fittest and all those old clichés. Well, I survived. Even though I was blind, I survived.'

'Without love?'

'It wasn't necessary.'

'No one can say that!'

'*I* say it!' He looked arrogant and challenging, his head thrown back, thumbs hooked into the belt of his trousers, his feet planted apart.

'Well——' she tried to look nonchalant, edging past him, 'then you certainly don't need *me*!'

'I said I *want* you,' he reminded her, hooking her back to him with a negligent arm, holding her easily against him. 'Not need—not love.'

His voice lowered and he caught her wrist as she pushed against him, holding it and curving his other arm tighter to stop her struggles. His lips brushed warmly on her temple and her cheek, sliding to her throat and into the opening of the caftan. 'You want love?' he murmured. 'Teach me, lovely Carissa. Teach me about love.'

She fought him, her will to resist strengthened by his cynicism, the mockery in his voice as he kissed her throat and shoulder, and brushed his lips teasingly against hers.

He went on touching her with his lips and his hands, and she knew he was waiting for the inevitable capitulation, and when it didn't come he kissed her mouth with savage anger, holding her still with a handful of her hair cruelly bunched in his fingers.

'*Let me go!*' she exclaimed fiercely when he lifted his head at last.

'Why? Stop fighting me, you little fool.'

'I *said*, let me go!'

He laughed, looking down at her furious face, holding her tautly resistant body with insulting ease. 'Make me,' he teased confidently.

He suddenly shifted his grip and swung her up into his arms, and was half-way up the stairs before she realised what he was about.

She hit at his face and kicked wildly, and he stopped and said in a hard voice, 'If you send us both down the stairs, there's no saying who might end up with a broken neck. I'm not letting you go.'

She subsided then until he reached the top, but as he kicked open the door of her bedroom, she raked her nails across his face, and had the satisfaction of seeing him wince before he dropped her on the bed and caught her flailing arms against it, holding her down.

He looked with narrowed eyes at her flushed, defiant rage, and said, 'Okay, I get the message. You don't want me right now.'

'I don't want you—*ever*!'

'There was a time when you weren't so choosy,' he drawled. 'I don't remember you insisting on love and promises in Sydney.'

Shock made her limp, suddenly. 'Sydney?' she repeated faintly.

'Eight years ago, wasn't it?' he said pleasantly. Then, with faint contempt, 'You haven't forgotten, Carissa. No girl forgets her first lover.'

She was silent with horror. She was so sure he hadn't remembered her, hadn't recalled her name, when they were introduced.

'Lost for words?' he jeered softly. 'Well, that's a change.'

'How long have you known?' she whispered. 'I thought—you'd forgotten. You never saw me.'

His voice hard, he said, 'I don't forget things like that. God knows I tried. Do you think I'd *forget* your name? *Carrie* didn't ring a bell, when Morris talked about you, but Carissa Martin certainly did. It's not a common name—you're the only girl I've known called Carissa. And the minute I heard your voice, I knew for sure.'

He stood up, and she put the back of one hand over her eyes, feeling shattered and vulnerable. 'You're one girl I remember very well,' he said.

She didn't hear him leave, but when she lowered her

hand, having overcome an urgent need to cry, he was gone.

It was a long time before she dragged herself from the bed to wash and change into night clothes, and the tears remained locked in her aching throat until she finally went to sleep, in the early hours of morning.

CHAPTER FIVE

IT might have been better if she had cried that night. Some of the tension within her might have been eased by it.

She was wary about Cade after that episode, knowing that when she showed it he was annoyed. She watched with trepidation the tightening of his mouth when she avoided any physical contact with him, the broodingly cynical look he gave her when she took a book from the shelf and sat as far from him as possible in the evening. They had been here nearly a week, and there was no word from Morris, and the angels reported no new developments, either.

On Sunday night, Carissa sat reading and Cade was staring out of the window at the other side of the room, into the swiftly falling dark.

'Come for a walk,' he said.

She turned a page composedly and said, 'No, thank you. You go.'

'I want you to come.'

She looked up with false calm and said, 'Sorry, I don't want to.'

She thought for a moment he was going to drop the subject, then he said, 'I understood you were here to entertain me and gratify my every wish—with the possible exception of one.'

She waited several seconds before putting her book down with an air of reluctance, and getting to her feet.

'I'm sorry, sir,' she said dulcetly, not caring that it would make him angry. 'Where would you like to go?'

His mouth tightened and a muscle moved in his jaw. She thought he might change his mind, but he said,

'Get a jacket or something. It gets chilly at night.'

It did sometimes, and she went upstairs and fetched a light wool shawl and tossed it about her shoulders, taking her time.

Cade had got a torch and instead of going to the lake he turned along one of the paths leading into the bush, leaving her to follow. But as they began to climb the slight slope between the tall totara, kahikatea and tawa, he took her arm in a firm hand, keeping her close by him.

A rabbit scampered away in front of them, white tail briefly flashing before it disappeared from the torchlight, and Carissa gave a small, breathy laugh.

'I haven't heard you laugh lately,' Cade commented.

'There hasn't been much to laugh about.'

They walked on in silence, and then Cade pushed her without haste but firmly on to a smooth-trunked log which had fallen near the path.

'I want to see the night life,' he said. 'Are there kiwis here?'

'Probably,' she said.

'Then perhaps we'll be lucky. Keep still and keep quiet.'

He switched off the torch, and they waited. At first she was conscious of nothing but the overwhelming darkness and the tingling awareness of her body to the presence of the man who sat with his arm loosely about her shoulders.

Then the small sounds of the night filtered into her consciousness—a faint rustling as a breeze or perhaps a nocturnal animal stirred the leaves overhead, the gentle creak of a swaying branch, a morepork calling mournfully far away, the occasional chirp of an insect nearby, and the dry stirring of the leaves that carpeted the forest floor.

Cade switched on the torch, transfixing an opossum in its beam, saucer-eyes staring yellow, bushy tail erect, its hand-like paws clutching a forest berry between them as it stared back at them.

Then it dropped the berry and leaped for the nearest tree, scampering up its trunk, long claws digging into the trunk as it scrambled out of sight.

A few minutes later another rabbit skittered into view, and loped off again quickly as Cade caught it in the torchlight. Then he turned the light on to the leaves at their feet and began idly turning them over with a stick. Carissa felt her skin prickle as she saw the first insects scurry away from the light, but after a few minutes she found herself fascinated by the evidence of teeming life under their feet. Busy beetles scurried back and forth, moths hovered here and there and darted off into the trees, ants tracked purposefully about their business, and a cicada grub emerged before their eyes from its long underground life to find a convenient tree to attach itself to while it worked on emerging from its skin and shaking its wings free for tomorrow's sun.

But when a two-inch brown weta crawled out from an overturned rotten branch at Cade's restless probing, she jumped up and said, 'Oh, please, Cade, let's go. I hate those things.'

'What is it?' he asked curiously.

'A weta. They jump—and they can bite. Don't touch it!'

'Okay,' he shrugged, and took her arm to lead her back down the path, shining the torch ahead of them.

'You haven't seen your kiwi,' she said.

'Maybe another time. Were you brought up in this sort of place?'

'Not exactly. I was born on a farm—there was a bit of bush on it. When I was ten we moved to Auckland. But we had lots of holidays in places like this. Lakes and beaches.'

'It's a good country for kids, isn't it?'

'I suppose it is.'

'There are good places for kids in America, too, I guess. Only I didn't see any of them until it was too late.'

'Too late for what?'

'For me.' He paused, then said, 'I was brought up on the streets of New York—the wrong side of them. I wouldn't want that for my kids.'

'Are you planning to have any?'

She thought he wasn't going to answer, but eventually he said, 'You mean, I'm putting the cart before the horse, don't you? The love and marriage bit comes first, *then* the kids?' He laughed, a short, harsh sound. 'You're a sentimentalist, aren't you? You didn't want to wear my "mother's" ring because marriage is sacred. Don't worry—Jack bought it, secondhand.'

Hurt and angry, Carissa was silent, and he didn't speak again either, until they were nearly out of the trees. Then he said, 'What about a moonlight swim?'

The lake rippled silver in the moonlight, and for a crazy moment she was tempted.

'I'm afraid it's too cold for me,' she said.

'*Is* it the cold that you're afraid of? Or is it me?'

'Of course I'm not afraid of you!'

'Then perhaps you should be.'

'Is that what you want?'

'To frighten you? No. You know what I want.'

'I can't oblige,' she said firmly.

'*Can't?*'

'Won't, then. I won't be another of your procession of adoring women,' she said bitterly.

He said coldly, 'But you already have been—once.'

'Once was enough. It wasn't an enjoyable experience,' she said bitterly.

For a few moments he was silent, and she had the idea that she had shaken him a little.

As they reached the door and he opened it, he slid

his hand under the shawl and touched her arm.

'You're not cold,' he said. 'Get your swimsuit.'

'Please—I don't feel like swimming.'

She blinked as he switched on the light, and he looked down at her face for a few moments. 'Then sit on the sand and keep me company,' he said. 'Will you?'

He took her by surprise, asking like that, instead of reminding her that pleasing him was part of her job. She nodded, and waited for him as he went upstairs to get changed.

He came down looking brown and masculine in dark swim shorts with a towelling robe slung over his shoulders, and she turned to fumble with the door handle so that she wouldn't stare.

They went out into the softness of the night, and she sat on the pale strip of sand while Cade splashed into the lake and created broken lights on the moon-glossed water.

A night breeze stirred her hair and lifted the tassels on the shawl, and she closed her eyes and rested her head on her raised knees in front of her, trying to make her mind a blank, to damp down a faint hint of regret that she had refused to join Cade in a swim. It would have been far too dangerous ...

She didn't know he had come out until a drop or two of cold water splashed on to the nape of her neck, and she looked up to find him towelling his hair. Water gleamed on his body and legs in the moonlight, and she was ashamed of the sudden wave of desire that warmed her body as she watched him.

He stooped to pick up the robe and fling it round his shoulders, then hooked the towel about his neck. Carissa stood up hastily and he said, 'You wouldn't like to dally in the moonlight for a while?'

'I want to have a hot drink and go to bed.' She

couldn't resist adding, 'Besides, aren't you forgetting your guardian angels?'

Surprisingly, she heard him laugh as they started back to the house. 'They wouldn't be likely to make that mistake twice.'

A few minutes later he caught at her arm, his fingers hurting her, and pulled her to a dead stop. She looked up questioningly, then followed his gaze to the shadows near the door, stiffening as one detached itself.

The next moment she found herself flung roughly on to the lawn, and a man's sharp voice said, 'Okay! It's *Pat!* Steady on, Mr Franklin.'

Struggling to her feet, she heard Cade say furiously, '*You bloody fool!* If I'd had a gun I'd have killed you. What the hell are you playing at?'

'We thought we heard someone at the gate. Didn't see anything, but I thought I'd better check out the house. You didn't lock the door.'

'Well, next time I will,' said Cade, not quite pleasantly. 'You're very conscientious, but I wish you'd shown yourself sooner and more clearly.'

'Didn't mean to give you a fright, sir. Sorry.'

In clipped tones, Cade said, 'Goodnight, Pat.'

'I'll hang about for a while, in case. Don't mind me.' Pat moved away into the darkness.

Carissa was standing on the lawn, conscious now that her side ached and she had grazed her forearm when Cade pushed her. Her shawl lay on the ground, and he came and picked it up, replacing it around her shoulders.

'Are you all right?' he asked.

'Yes.'

But he took her arm and she winced away from him, making him look at her sharply, then pull her into the house by her wrist. He locked the door behind them and turned to her when he had switched on the light.

'I only pushed you to keep you out of any trouble

coming my way,' he said, as though he had made some determined effort to speak calmly.

'I know.'

'Then why did you flinch away from me?' His eyes passed rapidly over her with suspicion, and then he flicked the shawl from her clutching fingers, and found a streak of blood on it.

'It's nothing,' she said. 'Just a grazed elbow, that's all.'

'Show me.' He didn't wait to be shown, but lifted her arm, revealing the bloodied, dirty-looking streak edged with green grass stains.

'It won't look nearly so bad when it's washed,' she assured him, watching his quick frown.

'You look pale,' he said. 'Are you hurt anywhere else?'

'No—at least, I expect I've a couple of bruises, but they'll heal.'

He half-carried her up the stairs, insisting on keeping his arm about her, and pushed her into the bathroom.

'Have a warm shower,' he said, 'and then I'll attend to that graze.'

She showered quickly, and since he had given her no chance to get a robe from her room, wrapped a towel about her and was trying to steel herself to come out of the bathroom like that, when he tapped on the door and opened it a fraction, to thrust her blue satin wrapper through the crack.

'Thank you,' she said, and took it.

When she went into the bedroom, tying the belt of the robe, he was standing there with a wad of cotton wool and a first aid box was open on the bedside table. He was fully dressed now.

'Sit here,' he said, and she obediently sat herself on the edge of the bed.

He tipped a bottle of yellow, strong-smelling disinfectant and liberally soaked the cotton wool with it, then pushed back the sleeve of her wrapper and began drawing it over the graze. He had even thought of putting a towel over her lap in case the disinfectant dripped.

It stung a bit, and he looked up sharply as she winced slightly. 'I'm sorry about this,' he murmured. 'I'm afraid in this case my reflexes were a little too sharp. I tend to react instinctively to danger—even if it is only imaginary.'

'I forgive you,' she said. 'It might not have been.'

'I wish you could be more forgiving about—other things,' he said, discarding the cotton wool and soaking a fresh piece. 'This may hurt a bit—there's dirt in the wound. I'm trying to clean it out.'

'Where did you learn to react to danger?' she asked. 'In that street gang you told me about?'

'And before. I spent most of my childhood in reform schools—no, it isn't what appears in the publicity handouts,' he said dryly, at her evident surprise. 'All that stuff about supporting my poor invalid mother and my baby sister was Jack's idea. You remember Jack?'

'Yes.' She hoped she sounded cool and casual. 'Is he still with you?'

'Couldn't do without him. He made Cadiz Fernand.' On an ironic note, he added, 'Without him, I'm not sure who I would be. Sometimes I wonder myself how much is real and what is Jack's fantasy.'

'No, you don't,' she contradicted him softly. 'You know exactly who you are. You always have.'

He paused in what he was doing and said, 'Do *you* know who I am?'

'I thought I did once, didn't I?' she admitted painfully. 'I was very young then—very stupid. You said so. And you were right.'

'You were also very sweet.'

He put down the cotton wool and picked up a piece of plaster dressing. 'Hold it steady,' he said, placing her arm where he could put on the plaster.

'Thank you,' she said as he took away the towel and closed the first aid box.'

'I'll get you that drink you wanted,' he said, and left the room.

She should put on something under the wrap, she supposed, but she couldn't be bothered. When he came back she had propped the pillows at the headboard of the bed, and was sitting against them with her legs curled up on the bed.

'Cocoa,' he said, handing her a steaming cup. 'All right?'

'Lovely, thank you.' She sipped it gratefully, trying not to notice that he stood only inches away, lazily watching her.

To break the silence, she asked, 'Is your mother still alive?'

'I don't think so,' he said unemotionally. 'If she was she would have turned up once I started making a name for myself—and money.' She looked up at him, and he said, 'I've shocked you. I haven't seen—I mean, my mother hasn't seen me since I was blinded—in a gang fight.'

'A gang fiight? I read——'

'One of Jack's stories, no doubt. The one about rescuing a friend from the wheels of a truck? I was never that soft-hearted.'

'Not even about your family?'

'What family? I never knew who my father was. I don't know if my mother even knew. There were lots of "uncles" in my young life, not much love. My mother was totally selfish. My sister ran away when she was thirteen. I have no idea where she is now. My mother —moved away while I was in hospital, and forgot to leave her address. All I had then was a guitar and a determination to crawl out of the gutter I was born into. Jack heard me playing and decided to help me do it—

for a reason. He thought we could go places together, and we did.'

So even Jack's motives were suspect, she realised. No wonder Cade said he had never learned to love.

His hand came out to take the empty cup from her as she finished the cocoa, and he stood holding it in his fingers. His hand was lean and brown, and she let her eyes travel up his arm and linger on the strong throat in the open shirt collar before reaching his face.

His eyes narrowed slightly, and he put the cup deliberately on the bedside table and sat down on the bed.

His hands slipped under her hair, framing her face, and he drew her close to him and kissed her gently. Carissa put her arms about him and snuggled close, then felt his mouth harden in passion as his hand pushed aside her robe and travelled with sure, caressing movements over the soft skin beneath. If there was passion, there was tenderness, too, in his touch, and she felt a surge of joy in the knowledge.

Then he suddenly thrust her away, saying violently, 'No! Damn you, not for pity!'

Automatically she pulled together the edges of the robe, demanding, 'What are you talking about?'

'You——' he said contemptuously. 'And your soft heart. Letting me make love to you because you see a poor motherless orphan who had a rough deal. Maybe I was once—but not any more. I'm a grown man, I'm big and I'm tough and I don't want pity. I want passion, and that's what I'm going to get from you—eventually. Not the fulfilment of a teenage fantasy, which you acted out last time, or a compassionate substitute for mother-love, such as you've just offered. I want you, Carissa, but on equal terms.'

'What terms, Cade?' she asked. 'Lust without love?'

He almost smiled, in a slightly devilish way. 'Call it

passion without prevarication,' he suggested. 'Or sexual honesty, to be blunt.'

'Call it what you like,' she said. 'I can't accept those terms.'

'You will.'

'No.'

He picked up the cup and balanced it in his fingers, standing and looking down at her, curled against the pillows, her fair hair spread about her, the robe still disarrayed, slipping off one shoulder, falling away from long, slender legs. His scrutiny was almost clinical, but a faint spark of desire still lit the dark eyes. '*Yés*,' he said, quietly implacable.

Carissa firmed her mouth defiantly and shook her head.

Their eyes clashed in silent combat, a tacit declaration of war.

Cade's smile held a hint of admiration, but it was confident of victory after a not unenjoyable struggle, rousing her anger and bringing a sparkle to her green eyes, before he gave her a sardonic nod and left the room.

The atmosphere subtly changed. Before there had been preliminary skirmishes with intervals of genuinely amicable truce. Now Carissa was constantly on guard against him, reminding herself that the most casual, friendly gesture could be part of his campaign to obtain her surrender.

Her suspicion was borne out by the expression she sometimes surprised in his eyes—a watchful, waiting look, as though he gauged her every reaction, was continually looking for ways of slipping under her guard.

Frankly determined to make her aware of him—and of herself—he made no attempt to hide the expression in his eyes when she emerged dripping from a swim in the lake, her swimsuit clinging to her tanned curves,

wet hair trailing across her shoulders so that she had to
lift it away from the curve of her breasts that the swimsuit left partially exposed.

Avoiding his eyes, she picked up her towel and vigor-
ously rubbed at the wet strands before sitting down on
the towel and taking a comb from the beach bag at her
side.

She turned her head away from Cade as she pulled
the comb through her hair, and she didn't know he had
moved until it was pulled from her grasp and his quiet
voice said, 'Let me.'

'No!' She turned sharply, making a grab for the
comb, but he held it away, the light in his eyes teasing.

'I insist!' he said. And when she reached again for
the comb in his hand, he smiled and said, 'You want to
fight me for it?'

Meeting the challenge in his eyes, she knew where
that could lead—a half-laughing, half-serious struggle
between two almost naked bodies, and he by far the
stronger ...

Defeated, she shrugged and turned her head away
from him. She hoped that her refusal of his challenge
had disappointed him.

The comb stroked into her hair, and she gritted her
teeth against the nearness of him behind her, the feel
of his fingers against her neck as he carefully combed
out the tangles. His touch was unexpectedly gentle,
patient and painstaking until every strand was smooth
as silk against her shoulders.

Expert, she reminded herself cynically, because he
had probably done it many times, for other women ...

The comb landed softly on the towel beside her, and
she felt his fingers part her hair at the nape, and then
the burning brand of his kiss on her neck.

Immediately she stiffened, and felt his hands clamp
on her shoulders to hold her.

New From

Harlequin

the leading publisher
of Romantic Fiction

What secrets lie within the Hotel De La Marine?

For weeks the small French fishing village of Port Royal had been aflame with rumors about the mysterious stranger. Why had he come? What was he after? Challenged by his haughty, yet haunted demeanor, Marie was determined to break through his mask of indifference. But he was as charming as he was cunning, uncanny in perception and driven by vengeance. From the moment she learned his secret, Marie lived with the fear of discovery, and the thrill of danger.

Uncover those secrets with Marie in the gripping pages of *High Wind in Brittany* by *Caroline Gayet* — one of the many best-selling authors of romantic suspense presented by Mystique Books.

MYSTIQUES

Now every month you can be spellbound by 4 exciting Mystique novels like these. You'll be swept away to casinos in Monte Carlo, ski chalets in the Alps, or mysterious ruins in Mexico. You'll experience the excitement of intrigue and the warmth of romance. Mystique novels are all written by internationally acclaimed, best-selling authors of romantic suspense.

Subscribe now! As a member of the Mystiques Subscription plan, you'll receive 4 books each month. Cancel anytime. And still keep your 4 FREE BOOKS!

'How frightened you are,' his voice mocked softly. 'Of me—or yourself?'

'I'm not frightened,' she denied. 'Just revolted!'

His fingers tightened momentarily, and he said with a hint of contempt, 'You liar, Carissa. You *need* a lesson in honesty.'

She tried to get up as his hands left her, but found herself grabbed and pinned down against the towel, her newly combed hair in a damp halo about her defiant face.

Poised above her, he said, 'You look like a virgin martyr, about to be ravished and thrown to the lions. Am I really a fate worse than death?'

He gave her no chance to answer, his mouth coming down with a suggestion of the ravishment he had talked of, a sensual attack with overtones of violence, forcing her lips apart and bruising their softness.

Carissa lay rigid, hating him for it, most of all hating him for the unwilling stirring of response he woke in her, which it took all her willpower to hide.

When his mouth finally stopped punishing hers, she was obscurely pleased to hear the long, unsteady breath he drew and see the flush of colour that darkened his tan. Even the light of anger in his eyes was an indication of his frustration and her success in hiding her feelings from him.

'You're not a virgin,' he said, 'for all your untouchable look. There must have been other men after me. And you're not as coldly indifferent as you pretend, so why hold out on me—why don't you take life as it comes, and enjoy it?'

'When rape is inevitable?' she quoted, with bitter mockery. 'That's a male chauvinist philosophy——'

Abruptly he twisted away from her, sitting up but turning his head to scorch her with furious eyes. 'I'm not talking about rape!' he snapped. 'I'll never force you, Carissa—I told you, equal terms.'

'And I told you I won't *meet* your terms!'

A glimmer of amusement lightened his anger. 'Then we seem to have reached deadlock—temporarily,' he said.

'Permanently,' Carissa said with decision.

He stood up, bringing her with him, with a slightly cruel hold on her wrist, and with a vicious little twist, brought her close. 'I wouldn't count on it,' he advised her quite pleasantly. 'Let's go in.'

There was a telephone call from Morris that evening. Carissa answered, to his rather guarded query as to how the honeymoon was going, that things were apparently peaceful, just as they had hoped for. His voice sounded familiar and safe, and with sudden hope she asked, 'Any chance of your coming to join us for a couple of days?' Oh, what a relief from tension that could be, she was thinking.

'Sorry,' said Morris. 'There's a lot to do here. My assistant left me to go on honeymoon, you know. I'm up to my eyes.' She couldn't join in his laughter at the feeble joke, and to stop herself from uncharacteristically snapping, she asked, 'Any other news, your end?'

'Well, that's why I rang, really.' His voice became confidential. 'Tell your husband that one of his birds is expected to be caged any day—but the—er—smaller one seems to have flown. Hasn't been seen for days.'

She smiled at his melodramatic way of putting things —she thought it highly unlikely that the phone could be tapped, and again had a strong suspicion that Morris rather enjoyed the excitement of this secret drama. 'I'll tell him,' she said, glancing up as Cade appeared, lounging in the doorway.

'And keep up your birdwatching,' Morris said mysteriously. 'There could be some—ah—exotic species about where you are.'

'We will,' she promised, her smile widening, in spite

of the serious implications of that. Morris's voice had
assumed a faint American accent, she noticed, and suddenly resembled that of a favourite actor in one of the
TV thriller series that she knew he was addicted to.

As Cade left the doorway and strolled over, to lean
on the wall by the phone, unashamedly listening,
Morris's voice reverted to normal.

'I hope this doesn't last long,' he said plaintively. 'I
miss you, Carrie.' She smiled, imagining him managing
without her assistance.

Cade's face subtly changed, and she realised he could
hear Morris's words now that he had reverted to a normal tone. 'I miss you, too, Morris,' she cooed softly.
'Would you like to speak to Cade? He's right here.'

'No, just pass on the message. Goodnight, Carrie.'

'Goodnight'—she waited for the click of the receiver
at the other end, and added—'darling.'

'That was Morris,' she said, hanging up.

'So I gathered.' Cade straightened, his eyes flicking
her face.

She walked before him into the lounge, saying over
her shoulder, 'He said to tell you that one bird is expected to be caged, any day, and the smaller one appears to have flown. Does that make sense?'

He didn't answer immediately and she turned to
look at him. He was standing in the doorway, a faint
frown between his brows. 'Yes, I think so,' he said at
last, coming into the room. 'It sounds as though the
police expect to get the gang boss—that's what they
hoped for, that my—attacker—would lead them eventually to the top man. But they've lost track of Gomez.'

'Gomez?' she queried.

'The one who's out for my blood.'

'Morris seemed to think he may be here. He said to
keep up our birdwatching.'

Cade gave a faint inclination of his head, then said,
'Anything else?'

'Not for you. The rest was—private.'

Her fictitious affair with Morris was a feeble defence, but the only one she had, apart from the flimsy barricades of her own stubborn will.

Cade suddenly walked over to her, and she turned her back, pretending to look out the window, pulling aside the curtain.

He said, 'Don't do that!' and pulled her away, his arm hard on her waist, holding her against him. 'Don't stand in a lighted window.'

She loosened his fingers with determined hands and moved away, but he caught at her hand. 'So you're missing Morris?' he drawled.

'Yes, of course.' She pulled against his hold, but his fingers tightened, and he raised her hand to his mouth and began kissing the tips of her fingers in a leisurely fashion that unexpectedly shook her. 'Won't I do instead?' he murmured, shooting her a wickedly sensual glance as his lips closed gently on the top of her thumb.

'No! *Stop it!*'

His teeth nipped the fleshy part of her thumb, then he raised his head and looked at her fully.

'That hurt!' she protested.

He laughed and caught at her chin as she tried to turn from him, pushing his own thumb between her lips. 'Pay me back, then,' he suggested softly. 'Tit for tat.'

Carissa wrenched her head away, profoundly disturbed and afraid of showing it. 'I'm not in the mood for childish games——'

'*Lovers*' games.'

'You're not my lover,' she managed. 'Morris is,' she lied desperately. 'And I think it's despicable of you to try to make love to me in his house, after what he's done for you!'

He let her go then, saying coldly, 'What he's done? What has he done? Tell me.'

'Well, brought you back here at risk to himself, and installed you in the lodge, given you a place to stay while the police track down this man who's out to kill you——'

'*Why?*' he snapped.

'*Why?*' she repeated, nonplussed.

'Yes—*why* has Morris been so—generous, so self-sacrificing, even to the point of taking the risk of sending his girl to stay with me on a fake honeymoon. I'll tell you why, my darling. Because he hopes and expects to be repaid in time, to the tune of a few thousand dollars in cash—when I repay his altruism by doing a concert tour for him. Right?'

'I suppose so,' she admitted reluctantly.

'Suppose? You *know* so. So what do I owe him, do you think? And you—do you think I don't know it was your idea he should tell me you were off limits? You forget, I have very acurate hearing—even now that I can see. Morris didn't want to put you out of bounds, Carissa. He wanted you to keep me happy. He was quite willing to throw you to the lion—wasn't he?'

'That's not true! Morris wouldn't expect me to——'

'Wouldn't he?' Cade's mouth was a bitter line. 'Stop pretending, Carissa. You know he wouldn't give a damn if you slept with me.'

That at least was true, and the knowledge must have shown in her face. Cade gave a hard little laugh, and said, 'Maybe it isn't the first time, at that.'

'What do you mean?' Her eyes searched his hard face.

'You've entertained people here before, for Morris, haven't you?' he said ruminatively, his eyes searching, speculating.

For a moment she looked utterly blank. Then as his meaning penetrated her brain, she was possessed by a spasm of blind, hot rage.

'How *dare* you!' Her voice was high and clear, and she hit out at him in a frantic fury.

He caught at her flailing fists and held her wrists in an iron-hard grip, twisting her away from him as she kicked out with her foot at his ankle, until she fell on the sofa, still fighting furiously, too angry to care that she had no hope of winning against his easy strength.

He held her down until she finally stopped trying to writhe out of his grasp, and lay panting and flushed, but still, against the cushions, eyes green as emeralds with a furious, impotent hatred.

'I take it I was wrong,' he said calmly. Then, unexpectedly, he added, 'I'm sorry, Carissa.'

He let her go and got up, walking over to the brick fireplace and leaning his hand on the mantel over it, looking away from her.

Her fury drained away, and she supposed it was reaction to that fierce emotion that made tears suddenly sting at her eyes. Horrified, she put up a hand to stop a sob, and when Cade turned to look at her she turned her face away, to bury it in a cushion.

She felt his hand on her shoulder, turning her to him, and this time her resistance was feeble, as he caught her to him with a gentle firmness that was new and surprisingly comforting, stroking her hair and whispering soothingly to her until the humiliating tears stopped falling. Even then she was content to keep resting against him, lulled by the soft stroking movement of his hands on her hair, and her back, the sound of his voice. His mouth brushed her temple and then her cheek, and when his hand moved softly to her face and lifted it so that he could kiss her damp eyelids, she didn't protest, only gave a soft little sigh that he captured suddenly and surely with his mouth on her parted lips.

The kiss was meltingly tender, then slowly, imperceptibly it changed to a languorous sensuousness, so that she didn't even recognise the slow heat that invaded her body as dangerous desire, it simply felt warm and wonderful, and her lips unconsciously clung, responding softly to his careful expertise.

His hand moved down from her back and began to stroke her thigh as he pressed her slowly down on to the cushions, and she felt him settle himself beside her, still holding her mouth under his, still evoking that pliant response.

His mouth lifted from hers and his fingers gently brushed away strands of hair from her throat, and he began to drop light, tantalising kisses on her throat, and into the open neck of her buttoned blouse.

Vaguely worried, she whispered his name, but he said, 'Shh!' and kissed her mouth again, discovering its contours, gently invasive. His fingers dealt with the buttons on her shirt and slipped inside it, and a sudden wave of astonished pleasure made her mouth open in a silent gasp, giving him freedom to explore it as he would, a freedom he took full advantage of.

With growing assurance he pulled her closer, laying the length of his body against her softness, allowing frank desire to harden his mouth on hers and direct his hands as they caressed her body.

She touched his hair tentatively, then let her fingers run across his shoulders. He took her hand in his and kissed the palm, then slipped it inside his shirt, and she opened her eyes as his smiled into them with glittering triumph.

She frowned and he said, 'Don't——' and smoothed the small lines with his lips, drawing back to look at her again. 'Don't worry, darling. You have beautiful eyes—so dark, so troubled.'

He made to kiss her again, but she moved restlessly and whispered, 'Cade, I don't want——'

He caught her face between his hands and contradicted huskily, 'Yes, you do.' He lowered his lips and kissed her slowly until he felt the slight resistance ebb away. 'You want me, don't you, lovely Carissa?'

Her eyes still closed, she felt drugged, and she dragged them open to see his dark, compelling eyes. '*Don't you?*' he insisted, a faint smile tugging at his mouth, removing its habitual bitterness, and tenderness tempering the demand in his words.

'Yes,' she admitted, helpless to defy him with a lie. 'But——'

'No buts,' he said, stopping her faint protest with his mouth on hers, kissing her into silence and submission, until she lay passive, her arms about his neck, her head tipped back against his arm.

But then he moved, pulling her up with him, still holding her in his arms, and said against her mouth, 'Come on, honey, it's nicer in a bed.'

Then she finally awoke from her passion-induced trance and pulled away from him, at first feebly, and then, as his hands hardened and tried to hold her, violently.

'No!' she said, and then more loudly, 'No, no, *no!*'

He took a deep, exasperated breath and said, 'I heard you the first time. I made a tactical error, didn't I? I should have taken you right here. You were far enough gone not to mind the discomfort.'

Knowing it was probably true, she said, 'That's a beastly thing to say!'

'But true,' he said callously. 'You want me—you said so.'

'That doesn't necessarily mean I'd let you——'

'You would have let me do anything—and that's the truth!' He reached for her and pulled her close, holding her shoulders. 'Isn't it?'

He waited for her answer, eyes blazing into hers. She didn't know, but defensively she said, 'You're very—

expert. That's exactly why I don't *want* you to make love to me.'

He raised a disbelieving eyebrow at that, and wearily she spelled it out for him. 'Not—with my *mind*,' she explained.

'And that's important?'

'To me, it is.'

'A meeting of minds—that's what you want of a love affair?' he asked with derision.

'I don't *want* a love affair—of any sort—with you!' she protested.

'Because I won't pretend that I love you.'

'Because you *don't* love me! Because you haven't ever loved any of the women in your life. They're all just a procession of faces, of bodies that you wanted for a time and then discarded when they no longer— amused you. Aren't they?'

He looked at her sombrely. 'No. Once that might have been nearly true. One does grow out of it. *I* did— eight years ago, when I first met you.'

For a minute she stared at him in sheer surprise. Then, suspicion making her angry, she choked out, 'That's a cheap lie!'

A muscle tightened in his jaw, and he said, 'How do you make that out?'

'You don't expect me to believe that? I might have then—but I'm not a naïve seventeen-year-old now! As you said,' she added with bitterness, 'a girl doesn't forget her first lover, but if you expect to persuade me to —to repeat the experience by pretending it meant something special to *you*, you can think again. I'm not that stupid!'

She turned from him and left the room, ignoring his tightlipped stare at her outburst, pretending not to hear as he said her name with a harsh, urgent tone in his voice. She fled to her own room, pacing restlessly to and fro for a time with her jaw aching from the rigid control she was exerting to stop herself from diving on to the bed and indulging in another fit of tears. He wasn't worth it, she kept telling herself fiercely, wishing her idiotic emotions would agree to being ruled by her head. He wasn't worth it.

CHAPTER SIX

CARISSA had to shop the next day—they were short of eggs and a fresh supply of bread was needed. She was relieved to be away from the lodge for a short time, and lingered in the shop, looking over the rack of magazines and finally picking out a couple to add to her purchases. A picture of a crocheted wall-hanging caught her eye on one of the covers, and she found the instructions and with the help of the friendly woman behind the counter picked out some yarn and a crochet hook from the small stock the store carried. Crochet was a skill she had learned from her mother as a child, but had not exercised for a long time. She felt the need to occupy herself in the evenings, now, and keep her mind on something other than the tension between herself and Cade.

There were several people in the shop by the time she had finished and picked up the large paper bag containing her purchases. One man, standing in front of the door, eyed her with considerable interest as she moved towards it, and she had to stop in front of him until, with a murmured apology and a smile, he moved aside to let her pass. He was dark, with a lean, intense-looking face and a wiry frame, a little taller than she was.

For a moment or two she felt uneasy, but she was used to being looked at by men, and decided that she had been made over-anxious by circumstances. She kept an eye on the rear-vision mirror on the way home, but saw no one until Pat on the motor-cycle loomed into view and eventually passed her, to stay just in front until he turned with a wave down the track to the fishing hut.

When she took out the wool and began to crochet a chain that evening, Cade eyed her with amused cynicism.

'How domesticated you look,' he drawled. 'Are you making something for me?'

'No.'

After a few moments he strolled over and looked over her shoulder at the magazine, open at the illustration and instructions she was following. The design was of stylised fish, two intertwined in graceful curves.

'Very nice,' Cade commented. 'Are you going to give it to Morris——? perhaps he'll hang it in his bedroom along with his prize trout.'

'Maybe,' she agreed.

It had been like that all day—Cade making mocking remarks that might have meant more than appeared on the surface, and Carissa answering with brief, noncommittal replies. She had hardly looked at him, but had been increasingly aware of his growing exasperation, the deepening of the sardonic lines about his mouth, the sharpening of his challenging eyes as he looked at her, the edge in his voice behind the lazy mockery.

Deftly she joined the edges of the chain and began to crochet into the circle, keeping her eyes on the hook as she looped in and out of the yarn. She wasn't fast, but the movements were coming back to her. If Cade didn't stand so close, she might begin to enjoy this in a mild way.

He suddenly swung away and went to the piano in one corner, picking out a tune with one finger, then sitting down and crashing into the opening bars of a noisy and passionate piece that she didn't recognise.

He played for a long time, switching from that to something quieter, and ending with some Lennon–McCartney tunes and then one she recognised as his own composition. His technique was not of concert standard, but she supposed he was getting something out of his system.

Apparently it wasn't enough. Abruptly he swung off the piano stool and said, 'I'm going for a walk.'

'Do you want me to come?' she asked composedly.

'Please yourself.'

'Then, if you don't mind, I'll stay here.'

'Naturally.'

He sounded fed up, and she pulled in her lips a little to hide a smile.

As he went to the door she said, 'Don't forget to tell your bodyguards where you're going.'

He stopped for a moment and then said savagely, 'The hell I will! I want to be alone—and I'll take my chances, thanks.'

She waited for a few minutes after the outer door had slammed behind him, then went to the telephone. Pat answered, and she said, 'Mr Franklin went for a walk. He said he didn't want company.'

'We'll keep an eye out,' the man promised.

'He isn't in a very good mood,' she warned.

Pat chuckled. 'Thanks for the warning. We'll try to keep out of the way.'

She thanked him and put down the phone. Cade would be furious, of course, if he knew she had phoned the angels. But it was her job, as well as theirs, to see that he came to no harm. And it worried her, thinking of him out there alone ...

She had gone up to bed by the time he came back, but she heard his key in the door and his footsteps coming up the darkened stairs, before she turned over and slept.

He was still restless the next day, and insisted on going out for a swim at the nearby hot springs. The bodyguards and Carissa tried to dissuade him, with no effect. He looked arrogant and determined and rather bored, and simply said he wasn't asking permission, he was informing them that he and Carissa were going swimming, and Pat and Stan could do what they liked about it.

As he put down the phone and turned away, Carissa looked at his implacable profile and said, 'And that goes for me too, I take it?' with a hint of opposition.

His eyes narrowed on her tilted chin and defiant eyes, and he said softly, 'You want a choice?'

Before she could answer, his hand whipped up and into her hair, pulling her close to his lean strength, and his lips were inches from hers as he said, 'Okay, we stay here and you—entertain me, or we go swimming, honey. To take my mind off my frustrations.' He lowered his head then, his lips barely brushing her mouth as he murmured, 'So—which is it to be?'

'You know,' she breathed against his tantalising mouth, trying to stiffen hers against temptation, pushing her hands against him.

For a moment he held her still, his eyes searing into hers, and then dropping to her mouth, until she whispered, 'You're hurting me!'

He was, but she didn't care about that, only couldn't stand the nearness of him any longer, deathly afraid that she would give herself away if he didn't stop holding her.

His hand dropped and she stepped back from him, taking a deep breath, saying, 'You don't leave me much option.' With sudden passion she added, 'There are times when I hate you—I could sympathise with that Gomez man.'

The water in the pool was deliciously warm, and a clean, sparkling blue. Carissa soon became accustomed to the faint smell of sulphur that overhung the area, and swam lazily from end to end, turning on her back to float, with the blue sky overhead filling her vision.

Until a dark, seal-wet head appeared beside her and

her pulses began to increase their tempo as he trod water beside her, his arm encircling her bare waist and drawing her with him to the side of the pool where he set her on her feet in water more than waist-deep.

He trapped her against the side, his hands on either side of her holding the surrounding rail. He was smiling, and her heart seemed to do peculiar things as she watched the change it brought to his harsh face, the deep creases in the lean cheeks, the slight softening of his penetrating eyes. She remembered when those eyes had been covered by dark lenses, when they had held none of the awareness, the life, that lit them now so vividly, and the knowledge brought a sweet pain.

Her face must have changed. Cade's stance altered, he seemed to lean a little towards her, and one brow rose questioningly.

She began to turn her head away from the enquiring look, but he moved one of his hands and gently turned her face back to him, asking, 'What is it?'

'Nothing. I'm just—glad you're not blind any more.'

Faint surprise showed in his eyes, and he dropped his hand. 'Me too,' he said, his eyes surveying her, a hint of tenderness in his smile.

Pat went by them, swimming with a ponderous crawl, and Carissa smiled at him. Cade turned his head, and she ducked quickly under his arm and swam away from him.

He came after her swiftly, grabbing at her ankle and then her waist, and she joined in the game joyously, splashing, fighting him off, but not in earnest, pushing at his sleek head when it came near, and wriggling wet limbs out of his grasp until he got his arms about her waist again and she gave up, gasping with laughter, her face against his shoulder, her hands slipping down his muscular arms.

'Give up?' he said teasingly in her ear, and she gasped, 'Yes, all right. Let go!'

She looked up, and he was looking back at her with an odd, arrested expression on his face, as though he had just noticed something about her he had never seen before.

Then he said, 'No.' But he did, and she floated away from him with a curiously flat feeling inside. Because she hadn't really wanted him to let go. She had wanted him to kiss her. She had wanted him to hold her for ever, and never let her go, and all the other extravagant desires that went with—love.

'Oh, no!' she whispered protestingly to herself. She couldn't be that crazy—could she?

She got out of the pool, throwing back wet hair as she did so, and almost collided with the man who had been in the shop the day before.

'Hello,' he said, with a soft American accent. 'We meet again.'

She smiled absently and walked by, too preoccupied with her disturbing new knowledge of herself to do more than barely notice him.

She spent a long time drying and dressing herself, combing her hair out carefully after towelling it with unnecessary force which she regretted when it came to pulling her comb through the resultant tangles.

When she came out Cade was already waiting for her, and she glimpsed Pat and Stan at the gateway of the pool area.

They drove back along a winding road round the lake, the bush thick as it tumbled down the bank on one side, occasionally receding behind small cottages, and the blue of the lake rippling on the other side.

Cade touched her hand with his and she pulled away, earning a hard glance and a mocking, 'Climbing back behind the barricades again, Carissa?'

She didn't answer, turning to watch a fisherman wade into the lake, and expertly cast into the deep water.

Swimming in warm mineral water was enervating, and she napped on her bed in the afternoon, but after their evening meal Cade insisted on going out again, and this time she went with him.

They stopped on a rise, the darkening water of the lake glistening at them through a gap in the trees, and listened to the night sounds, the small rustlings, subdued chirps and distant bird-calls.

'What's that?' Cade said quietly, moving his head. Carissa heard nothing at first, then the sound came again, and she said 'Kiwi—calling his name.'

He looked at her and suggested, 'Let's see if we can find him.'

They moved quietly through the trees, stopping every so often to locate the direction of the clear, whistling call. Cade covered the torch with his hand, allowing a minimum of light for them to see by.

Then they suddenly came on it, and Cade flashed the torch beam full on as the absurd bird, the egg-shaped body covered in long fur-like feathers, ridiculous little apologies for wings flapping uselessly in fright, its long curved beak poking agitatedly ahead of gleaming little eyes, fled from them precipitately on thick, long legs.

'You're lucky,' she said as the creature disappeared into the blackness among the trees. 'You've seen your kiwi.'

She stepped back, ready to turn and retrace their steps, and something rolled under her foot with a metallic thud and she flung out an arm to keep her balance, grazing her hand on a nearby tree.

Cade's hand grasped her other arm, steadying her, and he flashed the torch at their feet, revealing a beer can and several cigarette butts, white against the myriad browns of the forest floor.

Faint anger stirred at the thoughtlessness of people who littered the most beautiful places on earth with their carelessly thrown rubbish, before Cade shone the torch up and asked, 'Are you all right?'

'Yes,' she said, then noting a faint throbbing in her hand, she touched it with the fingers of the other and amended, 'At least, I think I've collected a splinter.'

'Let me see.'

She held out her hand to the light, and there it was, a nasty little sliver of rough wood, under the skin of her palm, on her right hand.

'It looks as though my first aid is required again,' said Cade. 'We'll go back and find some tweezers.'

'I'd pick up the litter first,' she said.

He took her arm and said, 'Another time. Let's go.'

Then he didn't move, and she laughed and said, 'We're lost—aren't we?' It was funny, his being so masterful about it, and then finding he didn't know which way to go.

'Shut up!' he said, quietly but with such sharpness that it stilled her laughter abruptly. With a spurt of anger, she said,

'Sorry, I'd forgotten what touchy egos you entertainers have.'

He said, 'The lake is over there,' and turned her to walk through the soft darkness until she saw the sparkle of the water in the moonlight. Had he seen it before her, or had his exceptionally sensitive hearing picked up the soft lapping of the water against the gentle shore?

But she didn't ask him, because he had shattered the more mellow mood they had shared for a while, and she felt faintly resentful. Besides, her hand was stinging and sore.

Once they found the shore it was easy to make their way back to the lodge.

Inside, she said, 'I'll manage,' and made for the bathroom, but Cade followed and insisted on drawing out the splinter for her and dousing it with disinfectant. He did it with a detached air that almost piqued her, so impersonal was his touch, and after he had pressed a piece of plaster over the small wound he left the room immediately, giving her an almost curt 'Goodnight.'

He had gone downstairs again, and she didn't hear him come up before she went to sleep.

His mood seemed to last over the next few days. He was inexplicably distant, almost absentminded, as though he was continually thinking about something else, and yet at the same time there was an underlying vigilance in him, a concealed alertness that showed when he whipped round his head at some small, unexpected sound, when he scanned the landscape with seeming casualness when they left the house. He spent quite a lot of time sitting on the verandah facing the lake, with a pair of binoculars lifted to his eyes.

With Cade's attention seemingly shifted from her, Carissa should have been relieved, but the atmosphere was still subtly tense, and she sometimes felt as though her nerves had reached screaming point.

She had been swimming alone in the lake, in the late afternoon, and was pulling a towelling robe about her when she saw a flight of red and green parakeets, about ten of them, alight nearby in the trees. Enchanted, she walked softly closer, trying to get a nearer look at them as they flitted about among the branches, the vivid scarlet feathers flashing.

She almost fell over the boat, drawn up across the sand and under the trees, before she saw it, because it had been covered with branches torn from the trees, the leaves slightly withered, but still green.

She stood staring down at it, her heart beating fast, it was so secretive, a boat hidden like that. Soft prickles of unease chased up her spine, and when a figure appeared among the trees nearby she jumped.

'Sorry—did I startle you?' The man looked so harmless, as he had in the shop when he had absentmindedly blocked the door, then apologetically stood aside, and at the pool when she had barely acknowledged his greeting, that she stopped her quick movement of flight and said with some breathlessness, 'Yes, you did, a bit. What are you doing here?'

He gestured to the binoculars hanging about his neck and said, 'Birdwatching. You too, huh?' He smiled. 'Those parakeets—they're worth watching, aren't they?'

'Yes. Is this your boat?'

'Yeah, sure. Anything wrong?'

'I wondered why it was—camouflaged.'

'Well, to fool the birds, naturally. Makes quite a good temporary hide, you see.'

She looked again, and did see that the branches were leaning towards each other, making a sort of tent over the boat, and that it would be easy to crawl in there and use it as a hide to observe the wild life without being seen.

'I'm afraid you're on private property here,' she told him.

'I am? Gee, I sure am sorry to hear that,' the man said, looking crestfallen. 'It belongs to—er—you and your husband?'

'Actually, to a friend,' she said. 'We have no authority to allow birdwatchers to use it, I'm afraid.'

'Oh, I understand,' he said. 'Guess I'd better move on out.' With obvious reluctance he began to move the greenery away from the boat.

'When did you move in?' she asked, wondering how the angels had missed seeing him.

'Oh, in the early hours of the morning,' the man said, throwing aside a branch. 'The best time to see the birds, you know, early morning. I set up when it was still dark, and waited.'

'You must have a lot of patience,' she said.

He shot a glance at her, then turned his attention to another branch, saying briefly, 'I have.'

She bent to help him, and said sharply, *What's that?*

There was a long, canvas-wrapped bundle in the bottom of the boat.

'My tripod,' the man said, casually. 'For my camera,' he explained.

'Oh, yes.' There was a rucksack stowed under the seat, and another square-looking canvas bag such as she had seen photographers using.

She helped him to push off into the water, and he waved at her as he rowed into the lake. She walked back along the sand, to find Stan coming towards her.

'Who's your friend?' he asked.

'No friend. Someone you missed last night,' she said. 'A birdwatcher—a genuine one.'

'You sure about that?'

'Well, I think so. He seemed very open. He came in last night—or rather, in the dark hours of the morning.'

'We patrol along the shore all night,' Stan told her.

'Maybe he slipped in between patrols.'

'Yeah—maybe. I don't like it, though. I wish your Mr Franklin was a bit less—independent.'

She smiled, guessing he would have liked to use a stronger word. 'He's restless,' she said. 'He doesn't like being—confined.'

She left him on the shore and turned to go back to the lodge, surprised to find that Cade had left the verandah and was standing on the wide lawn, sweeping the lake with his binoculars.

He lowered them as she came near, and asked, 'Where have you been?'

'Swimming,' she said. 'I told you——'

'You came out of the water twenty minutes ago,' he said harshly, stirring resentment in her with his accusing tone.

'I was watching some parakeets——' she began, stopping as she caught disbelief in his face. Perversely, she decided not to go on and tell him the rest. 'Do I have to account for my every movement to you?' she asked angrily, and brushing past, hurried into the house.

She had half expected him to follow, but he didn't. She supposed that Stan would tell him about the American, she was damned if she would.

She refused to go with him next day when he wanted to take the boat on the lake. They had been out in it once or twice, while Stan or Pat pretended to be fishing from their own runabout nearby, but she knew they didn't like the idea much. They felt it made Cade too visible and too vulnerable.

She sat in the shade of the verandah and watched as the boat nosed out of the inlet and into the lake, and relaxed slightly as she saw, several minutes later, the following wake of the angels' boat as they passed nearby.

There were several boats on the water, and at one end of the lake a water-skier was flying behind a roaring speedboat. Carissa was convinced that Cade would have liked to have that sort of speed just now, the thrill of power and the wind whipping through his hair as he skimmed over the water with the spray in his face. The outboard motor on Morris's small boat was capable of respectable but not thrilling speed.

She watched as he cut the engine almost dead in the middle of the lake, idling for a while before he turned the nose towards the shore again and began coming in slowly.

When the spurt of water suddenly leaped just in front of the boat, she thought it was a jumping trout. Then the sound of the rifle shot registered on her shocked ears, and she found herself up and running down the steps and across the lawn as another shot came and she saw Cade suddenly sprawl forward.

Still running, she screamed, '*No!*' and Cade's name as the boat seemed to suddenly leap forward, then turn as though out of control, taking an erratic course away from her. The other boat, with Stan and Pat in it, had passed Cade's, and she heard confused shouting above the snarl of the motors.

Her feet splashed into the water, and she stopped, sobbing with fear and frustration, trying to see what was going on out on the water.

The angels' boat had taken off across the water, pursuing a green speedboat that suddenly shot out from the cover of the trees. Then she saw with a tremendous surge of relief Cade's dark head come up as he steered the boat after them.

She was standing on the sand when they came back, with Pat in Cade's boat and Stan driving the other. They appeared subdued as they brought the boats into the sand.

She had dried her tears and tried to appear composed as Pat said, 'We lost him. The boat was hired, and no one knows where he came from. Well, the police will have to come into it now. There were witnesses to that little lot. The armed offenders' squad is on its way, but I don't think there's much chance they'll catch him—not in this country.'

'He knows where Cade is,' she said, keeping her eyes on Pat, on Stan, not looking at Cade at all.

'We're spending the night in the lodge, with you,' said Stan. 'And as soon as we have a police escort, we'll get you and Mr Franklin out of here.'

'We'll get our stuff and move in now,' Pat said. 'You two had better go to the house—and stay there.'

'We'll be ten minutes.' Stan added reassuringly. 'He can't get back here in that time.'

They moved off swiftly together, and for the first time Carissa looked at Cade's face. His eyes were glittering, and there was a narrow smile on his dark face.

He looked grimly exhilarated.

She thought of the tearing emotion that had brought her screaming to the water's edge when she had been so terrified that he might have been hit, and the long wait until he returned with the other two men. And in some perverse way he was obviously enjoying himself.

She took a long, shuddering breath, exclaimed, *'Damn you!'* And turned away from him, running for the house.

There was an air of siege about the lodge by the time the angels deposited sleeping bags and rucksacks and their incongruous fishing gear in the big lounge, and had gone round checking locks and windows.

'I never liked the idea of us being next door instead of right on the spot,' Pat grumbled. 'You're a stubborn man, Mr Franklin. I'm glad you've changed your mind at last.'

'There isn't much point in keeping up the pretence of a honeymoon any longer,' Cade admitted. 'Or pretending that you're anything other than—what you are.'

Carissa's accusing eyes met his enigmatic glance across the room. She had thought the idea of the two of them being here alone was Morris's or possibly mooted by the angels themselves. But apparently it was at Cade's suggestion—even at his insistence over the angels' better judgment.

The first contingent of police arrived more quickly than expected, by helicopter. The Inspector who questioned them all seemed to have a good deal of background knowledge already, and while two armed constables prowled around the house outside, he cast a disapproving eye at Pat's rifle and asked to see his licence, then took them all through their individual versions of the traumatic events of the afternoon.

'Any previous suspicious happenings, odd characters hanging about?' he asked.

'Someone has been lurking about in the bush near the house,' Cade said. 'He left cigarette ends and a beer can behind.'

Of course, Carissa thought. How stupid of her not to have realised. The butts must have been quite fresh, when she and Cade stumbled across them. They had been starkly white against the brown of the dead leaves.

'And then there was your birdwatcher,' said Pat, turning to Carissa.

She heard Cade's voice say softly, 'What bird-watcher?' and looked up to find his dark eyes intent on her face, his body tensely still.

Pat said, 'Didn't she mention it?'

Cade was still looking at her as he repeated, 'What birdwatcher?'

She wrenched her gaze away from his because it frightened her, and as calmly as she could told the Inspector about her encounter with the strange American who had said he was birdwatching.

Cade's hard stare unnerved her, and she stumbled once or twice over the words.

After the Inspector had gone she made a meal, glad of the presence of Stan and Pat, because she was still nervous of Cade, disliking the way he watched her.

She sat up late in the lounge, trying to concentrate on her crochet, while Cade strummed softly on his guitar and the other two periodically left the room to check that the house was still secure and to contact the two policemen still on duty outside.

It was almost midnight when she finally put down the hook and yarn and announced her intention of trying to get some sleep.

Cade rose too, and followed her up the stairs, making her heart thump as she tried to ignore his presence just behind her.

She was walking to her room when he caught her arm in a firm grip and said, 'Your room or mine?'

'*What?*'

'You heard.'

'What are you *talking* about?' she said sharply. 'We've never shared a room, and we're not starting now.'

'Yes, we are. I want you to hold my hand.'

'Very funny! This doesn't scare you in the least—you're enjoying it!'

'Aren't you?'

'*No!*'

'Well, maybe not. Things haven't quite gone as planned, have they?'

'No.'

'Never mind. Better luck next time. But don't think I'm going to hand you my head on a plate, *dear little schemer.* You're not going out of my sight until Gomez is safely locked up.'

For a moment she was stunned. Then as the implications sank in she said in a shaken voice, 'What on earth do you mean, Cade?'

'I like that innocent look,' he said critically. 'It's good. But too late. You shouldn't have let me see this afternoon how—chagrined you were that your friend had missed me.'

'*What?*' The shock was so great that she felt the hall in which they stood was moving, and she closed her eyes and swayed.

She heard Cade say roughly, 'Come in here,' and he shoved her into his own room and closed the door decisively behind them, releasing her arm.

'Cade, *please,*' she said breathlessly. 'This is crazy! You're quite wrong.'

'Am I? You have the whole night to convince me. Meantime, I'm taking no chances.'

'But, Cade, it's fantastic! How could I possibly have

any connection with Gomez?'

'I don't know how—but I know that he spoke to you when we went to the hot springs the other day. And I know you hoped I wouldn't find out about you meeting him yesterday. Did you arrange that at the pool?'

'I didn't arrange *anything*. Was *he* Gomez? Didn't you recognise him at the springs, then? You never said anything.'

'I didn't know then who he was. I wasn't sure until I saw him in the boat today. But I knew when I saw him pull out the other day after meeting you that it was the same man who spoke to you at the pool. And today I recognised him again. No wonder you wouldn't come in the boat today!'

'What exactly are you getting at?' she asked carefully.

'Somehow, you made contact with Gomez,' he said. 'Or he with you—perhaps that's more likely. He tracked me to here, saw you about the place and waylaid you on one of your shopping expeditions, perhaps.'

Carissa remembered then the incident in the shop when the man had stared at her so hard he forgot he was blocking the door, and to her horror she felt her cheeks grow hot.

Cade gave a softly unpleasant laugh and said, 'You're not a very clever actress, really, darling. You forget, the first time you fooled me so successfully I was blind.'

'It isn't true,' she said desperately. 'Anyway, *why* should I want to help him? *I* don't want you killed!'

'Then why did you conveniently forget to mention your little chat in the bush the other day with the birdwatcher? Why did you say *damn you*, when I arrived back safe and sound this afternoon? Why didn't you tell the Inspector you've met the man who shot at me more than once?'

'I didn't think it was important,' she said hopelessly. 'Cade, you can't believe any of this! What possible reason could I have for wanting to hurt you?'

'That's what I intend to find out,' he said. He moved towards her and she instinctively backed from him until she came up against the table at the side of the bed.

He stood in front of her, not touching her, but his very size and the cold anger she saw in his eyes was intimidating. 'Was it money?' he demanded. 'Or some kind of revenge? Do you hate me enough to want me dead, Carissa?'

'No!' Fear making her lash out with any weapon she could find, she said fiercely, 'You're paranoid! I don't hate you!'

His voice was so low it was almost a caress as he said, his eyes narrowing, dropping over her taut body, 'Don't you? Would you like to prove that?'

Her quick, choked, '*No!*' was cut off in her throat as hands closed on her shoulders and jerked her against his hard chest, and his mouth closed mercilessly on hers, giving her no chance to either respond or resist.

When he lifted his head at last, she ran her tongue over bruised lips and turned her head aside. His hands still gripped her shoulders, hurting them, and she whispered, white-faced, 'Please let me go.'

He released her and stepped back with a hard laugh. 'You can't take it, can you? Being kissed by the man you set up for a killer.'

'I didn't set you up,' she said wearily. 'But it's true I can't stand to be touched by a man who thinks I did.'

He looked at her narrowly, and for a moment she had a faint hope that he might believe in her innocence. Then he swung away from her to the chair by the window. 'You have the bed,' he said. 'I'll sit here.'

She hesitated, then slipped off her shoes and lay down on the bed. For a time she lay gazing at the ceiling. Then she said, 'If you think I'm—in some fantastic plot against you, why didn't you tell the policeman?'

'I have my reasons,' he said after a moment. 'Besides, I've no proof yet.'

'You're doing a lot of judging without proof, then,' she said bitterly.

'I haven't judged you yet,' he said. 'I'm just taking precautions—on a reasonable suspicion.'

'That's a matter of opinion.'

'A matter of life and death—mine.'

'Why does Gomez want to kill you?' she asked.

When he didn't answer, she went on, half nervous of him, half angry and intending to goad, 'It's a woman, isn't it? He wants to kill you because of a woman.'

'Sure,' his voice was closer, and she turned her head to see him coming to stand by the bed, looking down at her face against the pillow. 'Didn't he tell you?'

'Tell me what?'

He looked down at her, his face harsh and mocking, shadowed by the pool of light from the bedside lamp. 'That I seduced his wife,' he said, 'and then killed her.'

CHAPTER SEVEN

HER body seemed to grow cold as she stared at him, trying to read the truth behind the bitterness in his face.

'Are you admitting it?' she asked, finally, her voice barely above a whisper.

'God, no!' he said. 'I learned when I cut my eye teeth never to admit to anything.'

'I don't believe it,' she said flatly.

For a moment she thought surprise flared into his eyes. Then he said mockingly, 'Sweet of you. And in return I'm supposed to say I believe you when you say you don't know Gomez, right? Sorry, sweetheart, no deal.'

Furiously, she sat up and swung her legs to the floor, standing up to face him. 'You can't trust anyone, can you? You're so warped and twisted you don't believe in any sort of sincerity at all. I'm *sorry* for you, Cade! You may have talent and money and success, but you'll never have any of the things that really matter—love or friendship or trust—because you aren't capable of accepting them at their face value, you have to degrade everything with distrust and suspicion. You'll never have a worthwhile relationship with a woman because you aren't capable of giving a woman what she needs!'

She knew she had gone too far before he reached her, his eyes blazing fury as he pushed her down on the bed, hands as hard as steel on her wrists as he pinioned them beside her head, holding her down with his body as she struggled vainly against his angry strength.

'You think a woman needs love?' he jeered. 'Well, maybe I can't give her that—but how's this for a substitute?'

Carissa twisted her head to the side, trying to escape

his implacable mouth, but he found her lips anyway. She stiffened, expecting a second assault like the kiss he had forced on her before. But this was different—so different. He touched the corner of her mouth gently with his, then slid his lips across hers, lightly teasing, caressing, until she made an agitated movement of denial. But he wouldn't allow it. His mouth closed fully over hers, and his hand left her wrist to tangle in her hair and turn her head, holding it so that she could not escape. Her free hand pushed against his shoulders in a futile, mute protest, and then fell away, the fingers clenched in a desperate effort to stop them from stroking his hair or caressing the powerful muscles of his shoulders.

His other hand left hers and began a long, slow stroking movement down the length of her body, gently outlining the curve of her breast and hip, and his mouth continued its leisurely, seductive exploration of hers.

'Kiss me back,' he murmured against its softness. 'Hold me, honey.'

With an effort of will, she whispered, 'No,' and shook her head feebly, making a futile little effort to escape.

He stopped her easily, sliding his arms about her so that hers were imprisoned, taking her mouth possessively again, with passion and a hint of punishment, unleashing a hard sensuality that overwhelmed her and set every inch of her body afire with desperate need. His hands slid under her loose cotton blouse and one spread against her back while the other cupped her breast, pressing against its softness with firm warmth that roused her to feverish desire, so that without thought her arms moved to hold him closer, to meld her body into the hard contours of his.

His mouth left hers and moved, soft and warm, down the line of her throat, and his hand pushed aside her blouse—then she gasped a despairing protest as his mouth found the softness of her breast. It didn't move him, but a sharp tap on the door made them both tauten.

Cade swore softly and lifted his head, and Carissa moved sharply, pulling her clothes about her, as Pat's voice called, 'Everything all right, Mr Franklin?'

'Quite all right!' Cade answered sharply, rolling on to his back and watching with cynical eyes as Carissa, with flaming cheeks, fumbled at pushing her blouse back into place, and ran shaking fingers over her tumbled hair. She wondered if the angels knew how they protected *her*.

Pat's footsteps receded down the stair, and Cade's mouth twisted as Carissa made to get off the bed. 'Come here!' he muttered, and pulled her down across him. She struggled and he rolled over until she was pinned beneath him again. His kiss on her lips was short and savage and contemptuous.

'So I can't give you what you need?' he said derisively. 'Well, I sure as hell know how to give you what you *want*!'

He suddenly twisted away from her and left her lying, humiliated and emotionally exhausted, on the bed alone.

She had no answer for him, didn't want to look at him any more, it was too mortifying. She rolled over and buried her face in the pillow, wishing she could hide herself from him for ever.

From the window, he asked, 'Are you crying?' He sounded quite indifferent.

'No,' she said. She was beyond that.

She felt his presence by the bed, and without moving, she stiffened all over, every muscle contracting with tension, waiting. Then a blanket was pulled over her, adjusted round her shoulders, and Cade's voice, sounding strangely weary, said, 'Go to sleep.'

After a time, amazingly, she did.

Early in the morning Cade shook her awake. They were taken back to Auckland in a car driven by a policeman, with Carissa sitting beside him, and Cade in the back between two burly representatives of the law. Another police car preceded them, and Carissa looked out with weary eyes at the lush ferns and trees lining the road beside them as they made their way to the highway, and remembered the drive in the dark less than three weeks ago, reflecting bitterly on the changes in her since then.

Then, she had been nervous and worried, but reasonably confident in her ability to control her own emotions, to continue her full and interesting life after this slightly awkward interlude was over, and allow herself finally to forget the man who had shattered her young innocence so many years ago.

Now she knew that his attraction for her was as strong as ever—stronger, in fact. Her emotions were more mature, her physical responses more insistent than they had been then. She had been living with Cade in conditions of some intimacy for the last few weeks, and she knew herself now reluctantly but irrevocably in love with a man who admitted he didn't know how to love, who had no desire for any permanent, committed relationship with her or any woman.

She hardly noticed when they turned on to the highway and the bush began to thin and give way to steep hill-country with a scattering of sheep grazing the short grass, and then more rolling, gentler pastures and dairy farms with neat milking sheds and herds of black and white Friesian cows.

'Used to be all Jerseys, once,' the driver commented, breaking into Carissa's thoughts.

'What?'

'There used to be a lot of Jersey herds,' the man explained. 'Now it's mostly Friesians and these fancy new

breeds. Thing is, the dairy factories don't want too
much cream these days—they're making lots of skim
milk products for the overseas markets.'

'Oh, is that why?' she said vaguely. She caught
Cade's eyes on her in the mirror, faintly sardonic, and
made an effort to appear interested in the driver's
conversation. She didn't want Cade to guess at the
trend of her thoughts, and besides, she ought to make
the effort to take her own mind off them.

So for the rest of the journey she devoted herself to
entertaining the man, encouraging him to talk about
himself and making him feel that the things he told
her were of consuming interest to her. She learned
about his childhood on a dairy farm, his parents who
still worked the same farm, his ambition to join the
police force and how he had realised it, and she
laughed at his amusing stories of some of the episodes
that punctuated a policeman's life.

It was something she was good at, this drawing
people out to talk about themselves, a skill she had
cultivated and which was useful to her in her job.

There was little conversation in the rear seat, she
noticed. She was careful not to catch Cade's eye again.

When they drew up outside Morris's apartment, she
lingered for a few seconds to say goodbye to the young
driver while the other two men hurried with Cade still
between them into the building.

When she joined them, still with the traces of a smile
on her lips, Cade cast her a hard glance before turning
to Morris who was opening the door.

With her head high, Carissa joined the men in the
spacious lounge. Morris entertained a lot, and for a
town house, the place was roomy.

There was another man with Morris, who turned out
to be another Inspector. Apparently there were plans
to be made, more questions to be asked, things to be
discussed. To Carissa, who had wondered at the wisdom

of returning so ostentatiously escorted by police to Morris's place again, things began to fall into place. It seemed that they rather *wanted* Cade's pursuer to know where he was now. They hadn't found him at the lake, but a stolen car had crashed a police roadblock and been found abandoned further on down the road, and they rather thought the driver had managed to elude the police net and hitch a ride back to Auckland. A motorist had reported picking up a man answering to the description of Gomez. The idea now, she gathered, was to flush him out.

'By setting Cade up as decoy?' she asked, trying to keep indignation out of her voice.

Cade gave her another of his hard glances, and the Inspector said smoothly, 'He'll be quite safe, Miss Martin. There'll be plenty of us around, but we'll let him think we're a little—careless, and hope to catch him more or less in the act.'

'—Of killing Mr Fernand?' she asked.

'Not quite, but so that we can get him for attempted murder, which means a long sentence. We have circumstantial evidence that he was present, yesterday, but no one saw him shooting, or a gun. By the way,' he turned to Cade, 'you'll be glad to know they've got the big boss and most of his henchmen in custody. And our information is that the boss wiped his hands of your man some time ago—so he's on his own now. Once we have him you needn't worry that they'll send someone else to complete the job.'

'That's a relief,' said Cade, looking relaxed and lazy as he lounged in a chair. But his face was watchful and intelligent. 'Why did they dump Gomez?'

'Apparently because when the man the brotherhood sent to Melbourne bungled the job, Gomez took off against orders to do it for himself. His boss was annoyed—he'd been counting on having him there for another little thing that they were trying to pull off.'

The Inspector paused, then said, 'Our American colleagues hope that Gomez might be persuaded to give
evidence against the others—he has some inside information that they'd be glad to get hold of.'

'And that's another reason you want him to be up
for a long sentence, isn't it?' Cade suggested. 'So that
he'll be frightened enough to squeal.'

The big policeman pursed his lips, raised his eyebrows, then laughed. 'We like to help when we can,'
he said.

Cade stood up suddenly and strolled to the long
window, looking out into Morris's small walled patio.
'Gomez had gone straight for ten years before the
brotherhood approached him,' he said. 'Did you know
that?'

The policeman hesitated, then he asked, 'How do
you know that? Just because he didn't have a conviction for ten years it doesn't necessarily mean——'

'He was going straight,' Cade insisted. 'His wife told
me. She also said that he turned them down. They
were pressuring him to agree by threatening to hurt her
and their child.'

'Nasty methods,' the Inspector commented.

'*Did you know?*' Cade asked.

'Well—no. But I understood his wife was dead.
Wasn't that the reason that he wants to kill you? She
—er—died in your car, didn't she?'

'That's right. And Gomez joined the brotherhood
afterwards, hoping they would help him eliminate me.
His wife's death unbalanced him, Inspector.'

'The circumstances were—unfortunate,' the other
man admitted. 'But the man's a killer.'

'In some countries it would be termed a crime of
passion, and he'd get off lightly, even if he succeeded in
killing me.'

The Inspector smiled. 'You're not suggesting we
should let him, are you, sir?'

Wryly, Cade smiled. 'I have no desire to die. Nor much desire to exact vengeance on a man who's already suffered considerably. I tried several times to contact Gomez, to talk to him, before I left the States. He talked to me, on the phone, but only to threaten me and tell me what he thought of me. He wouldn't listen to what I had to say. Well, if I see him face to face, perhaps he'll listen. I don't like your idea, Inspector. I want your men called off.'

There was a surprised silence, then the Inspector said, 'Sorry, I can't do that. The man is wanted by the police both here and in the States.'

'Okay, that's your business. But I want police protection withdrawn from me.'

There was opposition from the police and from Morris, but Cade wore it down. He didn't want the police to protect him, and they could not force it.

After a slightly disgruntled Inspector left, Morris said, 'You can't stop them from watching the place from outside, you know.'

'I know,' Cade agreed. 'But if they stop him before he comes in they don't get what they want—a would-be murderer caught red-handed. And if they let him through, I have a fighting chance of making him see sense. Either way, I'm not their tethered goat.'

'Why bother?' Morris asked, a little plaintively.

Deliberately, Cade flicked a lightning glance at Carissa, who had sat silently in one of Morris's deep leather chairs all through the preceding arguments. Then he said, 'For the sake of his wife.'

Carissa spoke then. 'Salving your conscience, Cade?'

'Maybe.' His expression was enigmatic. 'I'll go to a hotel if you like, Morris.'

'No, no, you're welcome to stay here. I'll—er—keep you company. Carrie can go back to her apartment.'

'Carissa stays.'

Morris looked startled. He glanced at Carissa, who tried to look blank.

Cade said, 'You're both reasonably safe. Gomez isn't a professional killer, and if you keep out of the way he won't hurt you. It's me he wants.' He paused. 'I have no objection if you want to stick to your usual sleeping arrangements—I'm not easily shocked. But Carissa stays here.'

Morris, looking acutely uncomfortable, misinterpreted completely the pleading look that Carissa sent him. 'Carrie and I don't have that kind of arrangement,' he said. 'She'll have the spare room, and I'll toss you for the sofa.'

Cade's eyebrows rose. 'What—never?' His eyes slid to Carissa.

'Never.' Morris rose, glaring slightly, and said, 'I'll boil some water. It's the usual thing in a crisis, isn't it? Cup of tea, perhaps ...'

Carissa met the mixture of amusement and speculation in Cade's eyes with a defiant stare of her own.

'Never,' Cade repeated softly. 'Caught out again, my dear, deceiving little schemer! How well named you are.'

'Well, you jumped to conclusions,' she defended herself.

'Which you fostered—I wonder why?'

'I hoped it might keep you from pawing me!' she said tensely.

'Stop scratching, little cat. You'll get yourself in trouble.'

'Oh, *shut up*!'

'Who *do* you sleep with?'

'*No one!*' she flashed, adding hastily, 'At the moment. Who do *you* sleep with? Other men's wives?'

He tautened, but showed no other sign of anger. 'Not lately,' he drawled.

'What was her name?' she asked recklessly.

'Whose name?'

'Gomez's wife!' she said. 'Or can't you remember?'

'Yes, I remember. Her name was Carlotta. Why does it interest you?'

She shrugged. 'I'm interested in all kinds of things. It's part of my job. Small talk.'

'Oh, yes,' he said pleasantly, but with a cruel glint in his eyes. 'Small talk. Cows and farming and the policeman's lot with that young cop, in the car. Other men's wives with me.'

'On the whole, I think the cows were more interesting,' she said.

'Or the policeman?' he taunted. 'Did you make a date to see him again?'

'Don't be silly. We were only making conversation in the car to pass the time.'

Morris put his head round the door to enquire, 'Tea or coffee?'

Carissa got up and said, 'I'll come and help you.' She hadn't asked Cade the question that was burning on her tongue—*did you love Carlotta?* But she knew what the answer would have been. Cade loved no one. Then why was he prepared to risk his life to try and help Carlotta's husband? Because that was what he intended to do.

Did he have a guilty conscience?'

She pictured Carlotta to herself—it was a pretty name, dark, exciting, Spanish. Would that have described the woman, too? Another of the foolish questions she would have liked to ask Cade. *Was she pretty?* Of course she had been pretty. Cade's women always were, she reminded herself, deliberately.

Carlotta had died in his car, the policeman had said. An accident, then. With Cade driving. Obviously, her husband believed him responsible. With sudden pain, she wondered if Cade blamed himself, too. Was that why he had said he wanted to talk to Gomez for his wife's sake? Because he owed it to Carlotta, whose death he had caused?

She took him his cup of coffee while Morris followed with a plate of toast and cheese, and they sat eating and drinking with a false air of normality. Morris seemed to have conquered an initial nervousness and was full of businesslike plans for sharing a night watch with Cade.

When the cups were emptied Carissa collected them and took them to the kitchen, finding Cade behind her as she put them into the sink and poured hot water and detergent over them. In the events of the day she had almost forgotten that he didn't trust her. The sudden reminder was surprisingly painful.

In a brittle voice she enquired, 'Did you think I'd slip out the back door? Or wave a tea-towel to signal my accomplice, perhaps?'

'Perhaps,' he agreed, with a hint of amusement lightening the grim note in his voice. He surprised her by taking a tea-towel and drying up with quiet competence. The small domestic chore was so at variance with his fantastic suspicions of her and the whole wildly unlikely situation that for a moment she was tempted into hysterical laughter, a small strangled gasp of mirth escaping before she could stop herself.

Cade looked at her sharply and asked, 'What's so funny?'

'I couldn't possibly explain,' she said. 'It isn't really funny, anyway.' Nothing was funny, when she remembered that someone wanted to kill Cade, and that he had arbitrarily told the police to keep off. Carlotta being dead wasn't funny, either.

Something else that the policeman had said recurred to her, and she asked, 'What happened to Carlotta's child?'

'She's probably with her grandmother. Carlotta left her with her own mother when she came to see me.'

Stiffly, wishing she had never brought the subject up, Carissa said, 'I see.' Of course the woman wouldn't have brought her small daughter with her on her visits to her lover. She supposed Cade had never seen the child, and had no interest in her.

'More small talk?' Cade mocked. 'What else would you like to know?'

'I was merely concerned about the child,' she said. 'I happen to like children and have this notion that it's up to the adults of this world to care about them when they're getting a raw deal.'

He was silent, and she looked up to find him regarding her with an unreadable look. Uncharacteristically, he looked away again immediately and continued with his self-imposed task.

Carissa pulled the plug and watched the sudsy water disappear down the drain. It promised, she thought, to be another long night.

Carissa would have liked to go to her room early, if not to sleep, at least to remove herself from the tension of being with Cade. But when she made a move he forestalled her by smoothly suggesting a game of chess, with a glint in his eye that warned her she had better accept. They had played once or twice at the lodge, and Morris displayed a handsome chess set on one of the low tables in the lounge.

Morris watched for a while, then said he would go to bed and take his turn at going on watch after midnight.

When he had gone, Carissa pushed the board away and said, 'Are you going to keep me up all night?'

'Are you tired?'

'Yes. It's been a rough day.'

'All right, go to bed. Leave your door open—and remember I have very good hearing.'

She left the door ajar and climbed into bed after a

quick wash, and an equally quick change into a cool silky nightdress. She had switched off the light and was lying on her back, contemplating the darkness with depression and foreboding, when the door swung open and subdued light from the lounge behind him outlined Cade's dark figure.

Sitting up, she pushed herself back on the pillows and hissed, 'What do you want?'

'Just checking,' he murmured. 'You haven't moved for five minutes.'

'Oh—*go away!*' she said fiercely, turning her back on him and her face into the pillow.

She heard him move, but not away—instead he was crossing the room to her window, and as she rolled over to watch him he turned and came over to the bed.

'Go away!' she whispered.

'I'm not going to touch you,' he said with faint contempt, and sat down on the side of the bed, his hand coming down on the other side of her.

'If you do, I'll scream,' she told him. 'For Morris—and the police.'

'Don't threaten me,' he said on a warning note. 'And stop panicking. I said I won't touch you.'

'I'm not panicking,' she snapped. 'You don't frighten me!'

'Don't I!' His brief smile, white in the shadowed dark, seemed to disbelieve her. 'Then it's something else that makes you nervous of me.'

'I don't know what you're talking about.'

'Just the difference between *you* and Morris's description of his cool, capable, unflappable assistant. With me you tend to be emotional, highly-strung, rather volatile. One moment you're a passionate, tantalising woman, the next a frightened little girl, or a spitting cat.'

'I'm sorry,' she said stiffly, 'if I haven't lived up to

what Morris told you about me. If you're disappointed, I——'

'Oh, I wouldn't say that! I find it rather—exciting,' he told her.

She was silent, fighting a sudden wave of excitement of her own; the darkness about them seemed alive, enveloping the two of them in a warm intimate embrace, a heightened awareness of each other. He hadn't moved, but she felt suddenly that he was closer to her, and his voice came softly, persuasively. 'Tell me the truth about something, Carissa.'

'Do you think I can?' she asked, gently bitter.

He waited before he spoke again, then asked quietly, 'How have you thought of me, in the past eight years? With hatred? Because I didn't live up to your fantasy —oh, I know I was cruel. It was a new experience for me, too, you see. The only time in my life I've ever made love to a virgin.'

So he hadn't been entirely lying when he said she was special.

'Did it bother you?' she asked.

'You know it did. That's why I was so rough on you. I felt guilty—can't you understand that?'

Carissa was silent, and he said, 'You haven't answered my question.'

'I've tried not to think of you at all,' she told him. 'There was nothing I wanted to remember.'

'Nothing?'

'What should there be?' she cried softly. 'Shame, humiliation—pain? Why should I want to remember?'

Cade was perfectly still, but she had the sudden conviction she had shocked him. 'I'm sorry,' he said in a strained voice. 'If you'd been older it would have been easier to remedy that. Or if I'd known before——' He stopped, and said with faint harshness, 'I hope your next lover proved more—satisfactory.'

'What next lover?' she said bitterly, suddenly sick of

the pretence. 'I've had no other lovers.'

He drew in a sharp breath and leaned over to switch on the bedside light. *'What?'*

She turned away from the blaze of light, from his eyes, closing hers. 'There's been no one,' she said wearily. 'Never anyone but you.'

She felt his appalled gaze on her face, but couldn't look at him.

'Did I hurt you so much?' he said. Then, bleakly: 'My God, no wonder you hate me.'

His weight left the bed and the light snapped off. She heard him leave the room, and flung an arm up over her eyes as slow, hot tears trickled on to the pillow.

CHAPTER EIGHT

Some sound must have wakened her, and her eyes flew open in sudden fear as she saw the bulky figure near the window, silhouetted against the light from a street lamp that filtered through the curtains. The light suddenly blinked out, leaving the room in utter blackness except for a bright sliver that edged into it from the nearly closed door.

'Cade?' she whispered at the nearly invisible figure.

The man moved suddenly, with such nervous haste that she knew it wasn't Cade—or Morris. She threw back the blankets, scrambling for the door, screaming, 'Cade!' And the man lunged and caught her, pinning her flailing arms, hauling her backwards against him as she came off the bed, stopping her frantic struggles with a soft-voiced warning in vaguely familiar accents: 'I've got a knife here, girl. Shut up and keep still.'

And when Cade snapped on the light and flung the door open, with Morris, dishevelled and bleary-eyed behind him, Gomez had her in front of him, the slim, wicked blade poised at her throat.

Cade stopped dead, and Morris began to retreat hastily, muttering, 'Phone——'

'*Phone anyone and she's dead!*' snarled Gomez, and Morris paled and stopped uncertainly in his tracks.

Cade looked taut and furious. 'Leave her alone, Gomez! You've nothing against her. Only me.'

He made a move forward, and Gomez jerked the knife suddenly until Carissa felt its cold menace on her skin, barely touching.

Cade stopped, his face pale, eyes dangerous. 'You hurt her, *in any way*, Gomez, and I won't hand you over to the cops. I'll personally kill you, and it won't be easily.'

'Your girl, is she?' the man asked meaningly, and Cade's face was suddenly shuttered.

'She's just a girl,' he said. 'She's got nothing to do with what's between you and me, that's all.'

The man's breath was hot on Carissa's cheek as he said softly, 'I think she's your girl.'

'No,' she said. 'He thinks I've been helping you, Mr Gomez.'

She felt a momentary loosening of his hold, but it didn't last long enough for her to take advantage of it. She wondered if the Inspector had deliberately allowed Gomez to enter the flat or if he had eluded them. If they knew he was here, surely before long they would come ...

'Why should she help me?' the man asked Cade, sneeringly.

'Because she's another person who hates me,' Cade said calmly. 'Let her go.' Carissa saw Morris trying unsuccessfully to look blank.

'You must think I'm stupid!' said Gomez. 'She was with you at the lake.'

Morris intervened. 'She works for me,' he said. 'It wasn't *her* idea to accompany him. Or his.'

'You came to get *me*, Gomez,' said Cade. 'So stop hiding behind a woman——'

'I'm not hiding.'

'*Using* her, then—the way you used Carlotta.'

The arm about Carissa tightened with tension, and she felt the angry breath that the man drew behind her.

Cade went on, tauntingly, 'You used your wife, didn't you, Gomez? You sent her to me—told her to sell her lovely body to me——'

The man let out a mindless, inarticulate sound that was almost animal in its rage and pain, and Carissa was pushed aside as he launched himself at Cade.

Morris ran forward as Cade seemed about to crouch, then swiftly kicked upwards at the hand holding the knife. 'Keep out of it, Morris!' he growled, dodging in under the descending knife and grabbing Gomez's wrist with both his hands, giving a twist that sent the man to the floor. Cade moved again with unbelievable speed, half standing, and somehow the knife was in his hand, and Gomez lay spreadeagled on the floor, staring with impotent hatred into the glittering dark eyes above him as Cade held the knife inches from him.

Cade said quietly, 'Now—up, Gomez. Slowly. You and I are going to talk.'

Someone was hammering on the outer door, Carissa realised. Morris made an uncertain movement and Cade said, 'Tell the Inspector everything is under control, and *don't open the door.*' To Gomez, he said, as the man rose, his wary eyes on the knife in Cade's hand, 'Into the other room, and sit down.'

The policemen on the other side of the door argued, but at Cade's insistence Morris was adamant. 'Tell him no one comes in without a search warrant,' Cade ordered. 'And if they break down the door there'll be claims for damage and trespass that'll lose the Inspector his job.'

He had Gomez sitting in a chair, and he seated himself not far away, still holding the knife. Carissa had slipped on a wrap and was standing at the doorway of her bedroom, her hands unconsciously clutching at the thin fabric that crossed at her waist. Without taking his eyes from Gomez, Cade asked, 'Are you all right, Carissa?'

'Yes.' She hoped he wasn't going to make her go away. Gomez might be quiet and still, now, but he was flicking glances at that knife in a way that made her certain he was only waiting for a chance to take it again and finish what he had come to do.

Morris said, 'They say they've got a warrant, and if we don't open up they'll prosecute me for harbouring a criminal.'

'Cade——' Carissa protested, 'let them take him away.'

'No. Ask them to give me half an hour,' said Cade.

There was more calling through the door, and Morris promised to open it in half an hour. Cade said, 'Morris, if you want to leave, it's up to you.'

Morris shook his head, and Cade said, 'Carissa?'

'I'll stay,' she said.

'Would one of you get Mr Gomez a drink?' he said.

Morris poured some whisky, which the man eyed with suspicion, then drank at a gulp.

'Do you smoke?' Cade asked.

Gomez shook his head. Amazingly, he looked no different from the day he had convinced Carissa he was just a harmless birdwatcher, at the lake.

Cade said quietly, 'I apologise for what I said about your wife, it was the only way I could think of to get you to go for me. She came to see me of her own accord——'

He was stopped by a string of names from Gomez that made Carissa blink. Cade simply sat with an expressionless face until the man ran out of abuse.

'Now shut up and listen for a change,' he said, with a steely note in his voice. 'You are insulting your wife's memory, Gomez. She was never my mistress, and you should be ashamed of yourself for even thinking she would ever be disloyal to you. She loved you, that's why she came and asked me for money——'

'Why should you give her money—*for nothing*?' Gomez shouted. 'I saw the cheque she had on her when she died. Thousands of dollars! You paid her off, didn't you? Got sick of her and paid her off!'

'No!' Cade leaned forward. 'I knew Carlotta when we were both barely more than children—she was a

friend of my sister. Well, I lost touch with her—and
with my sister. But my name was in the news, Carlotta
knew where to find me. She came and told me that she
needed money—a lot of it, to get away to another
state and start a new life, with you and your daughter.
She was afraid for you, Gomez. Afraid that you would
be forced to work for the brotherhood, that her
daughter would have a criminal father, that you would
be involved in crime again, maybe caught. She was
desperate, and I was the only source she could think of
for the kind of money that was needed.'

'So you gave it to her—just like that? You expect me
to believe that? Then what was she doing in your car,
eh? When you crashed it and killed her?'

'It was an accident, Gomez. The other driver was at
fault—he'd been drinking, he was going too fast, the
car came round a bend and went out of control. You
must have been told that by the police——'

'Police! They protect the people with the money——
Did you kill her on purpose? Did you write that
cheque and then kill her so she could never use it?'

'Don't be insane! My manager and I were lucky to
get out of the wreck with our lives. We both spent some
time in hospital. Carlotta was in the front passenger
seat—she got the worst of it, and I'm very sorry. But
I can't bring her back to life for you. No one can.'

Carissa caught her breath at the torment in the
man's eyes as he looked up at Cade. More gently, Cade
said, 'We were taking her home—to you. We had to go
to a recording session and were going to drop her on the
way. She intended to pick your daughter up and then
go home and tell you the good news. A new life for all
of you. I'm sorry.'

The man was silent, glaring.

'It's true,' Cade insisted. 'I swear it's true. Carlotta
came to me asking for help for old times' sake. I gave
it to her. And all she gave me in return was her thanks.'

'Why?' Gomez asked gratingly. 'Why should you do that for her?'

Cade hesitated for the first time. 'Because once she was my sister's friend,' he said. 'I haven't heard from my sister since she ran away at thirteen. Maybe she's dead, I don't know. I made my name and my money too late to help my little sister, Mr Gomez, but I know she would have wanted me to help Carlotta. That's why.'

Gomez was shaking his head, but the look on his face was bewildered rather than rejecting. 'No,' he said. 'No. I can't believe it.'

'You'd rather believe your wife was selling herself to the highest bidder?' Cade asked coldly.

The man jumped up, pushing himself to his feet and forward in one swift movement. But Cade was up, too, moving to one side, the knife held in readiness in his hand.

Carissa had automatically moved, too, coming closer in some futile but instinctive desire to support Cade. As the two men faced each other, she said shakily, 'Please, Mr Gomez, can't you see he's telling you the truth? You loved your wife—you don't really believe that of her. You're angry because she's dead. But it's no use being angry. It wasn't Cade's fault. It wasn't yours. Nobody's to blame, Mr Gomez.'

He suddenly looked at her for the first time, then he collapsed on to the chair he had just left, burying his head in his hands, his breath coming in great painful gasps.

'I know,' he said. 'I know, I know.'

Cade threw down the knife on the coffee table nearby, and Gomez didn't even glance at it. Carissa moved forward and went on her knees beside the man's chair, her hand on his knee. He took it in his, clutching at her fingers, and looking at her said painfully, as though explaining something important to her, 'She was so beautiful, my wife—Carlotta. She's too beautiful to be dead.'

'I'm so sorry,' she whispered, swallowing a lump in her throat at the agony in his eyes. 'Does your little girl look like her?'

He nodded, the agony fading a fraction. 'Rita—yes. She's—she's like her mother. She misses her, you know.'

'She'll be missing you, too,' said Carissa. 'Shouldn't you be getting back to her? Carlotta would want you to be with her—wouldn't she?'

'Yes. But I've been stupid. I guess the child will be okay with her grandmother, until—until I get out of jail.' He took a long, deep breath, and looked up at Cade. 'Guess you'd better open that door.'

'Open the door, Morris,' said Cade. 'And tell the Inspector Mr Gomez would like to talk to him.'

The Inspector looked more than a trifle put out, and even more so when he had issued the conventional police warning to Gomez, and Cade enquired smoothly, 'May I ask on what charges you intend to hold my friend Mr Gomez, Inspector?'

'*Friend?*' the Inspector barked in astonishment.

'Perhaps I should make it clear Mr Gomez is here at my invitation,' Cade said patiently.

'Invitation? So he sneaks through a forced window, armed with a knife?'

'You mean *this*?' Cade negligently picked up the knife from the table and fingered it. 'This is mine, Inspector—a gift from a friend. You'll find my fingerprints all over it, if you care to check.'

Tight-lipped, the Inspector said, 'No doubt. Do I take it you don't intend to press charges of trying to murder you, either today or by shooting at you yesterday?'

'Attempted murder? That's a serious charge, Inspector. I wouldn't dare accuse anyone of that unless I had very good evidence.'

'Neither would I, Mr—Franklin. We have witnesses who heard the shots.'

'I wasn't shot, Inspector. Even the boat is unmarked.'

'They also saw the man trying to evade you and your—bodyguards.'

'How many saw the man's face? We lost him, Inspector, unfortunately. Disappeared into thin air, apparently—never saw him again. Some crazy guy, duck-shooting, maybe, careless with his gun.'

'I could subpoena you, Mr Franklin. And your two friends.'

'You could, but I'd be an unco-operative witness. On the other hand, I think you'll find Mr Gomez quite co-operative, on the subject of a matter of great interest to your colleagues back in my home state. He has a little girl back there, you know, and an interest in keeping certain characters away from her. By the way,' he added, turning to the man now standing between two burly policemen, 'you never used that cheque. I'll be happy if you would accept another—for your little girl's sake, to help you move her to another state. For my sister's sake.'

'Thanks,' the man said huskily.

'Sister?' the policeman queried sharply. 'Was Gomez's wife your sister?' he asked Cade suspiciously.

'You're quick, Inspector, but wrong,' Cade said. 'No.' His eyes went to Gomez. 'But I wish she had been. I would have been proud of her.'

It seemed to Carissa that the last remnant of suspicion disappeared from Gomez's eyes then.

They took him away, and Morris threw himself on the sofa and let out a long whistle of relief.

Suddenly finding her legs threatening to give way, Carissa sank down on the nearest deep chair.

'Are you all right?' Cade asked her.

'Yes. But I could do with a drink.'

Morris got up and poured for them all.

They drank in silence, Cade still toying with the knife, its wicked blade shimmering in the light.

'I wish you would put that thing down!' she said, finding her voice wavering.

'Sorry.' Cade put it back on the table. 'He wouldn't have hurt you, you know. He's not a genuine killer.'

'You were sorry for him, weren't you?' she said, remembering he had told her he had never been soft-hearted.

He cast a sharp glance at her and said, 'Let's postpone the post-mortem, shall we? I want some sleep.'

'Me too.' Morris yawned, and said, 'The couch is all yours, Cade.' He disappeared into his room, and Carissa put the glasses away in the kitchen and came back to go through to the spare room.

Cade was still sitting in a chair, and he had the knife in his fingers again.

'Are you going to keep it for a souvenir?' she enquired, a little sharply.

'Maybe.' His fingers stilled, and he looked at her as she stopped in the doorway to the bedroom.

'I'm sorry I didn't trust you,' he said. 'If it helps any, I wanted to, badly. But——'

'But you don't trust anyone,' she said. 'I know. Especially me.'

In the morning she woke late, feeling somewhat depressed and flat. The strain was over, and that should have been a relief, but all she could think of was that Cade would be going away again, and she would become again just one of the girls he had loved a little and then left.

She tried to rally her self-respect with the thought that this time he had not taken all he wanted from her, that he had lost the battle of wits to which he had challenged her. If it was a victory, it felt like a hollow one. He had wanted her, in a physical sense, and she had refused him that. But she wanted him too, in far more than a physical way, and the pain of losing him was a deeper and more lasting one than any chagrin he would suffer at her refusal to gratify his fleeting interest in her.

When she braced herself to get up and dressed and emerge into the lounge, it was to find Morris there alone.

'Cade went to the police station,' he told her. 'He asked me to find the best lawyer in town and he's taken him to see Gomez himself. He really wants to help that guy. Do you know what I think?'

'What?' Carissa asked vaguely, trying to assimilate simultaneous feelings of relief and disappointment that Cade wasn't there.

'I think he did have something going with that Carlotta. Why else would he go to the trouble that he has, to get her husband off the hook? After all, the guy *was* trying to kill him!'

'Perhaps he just felt guilty about Carlotta being killed when he was driving,' Carissa suggested, trying to hide her misery at the thought that Morris voiced.

'But he wasn't driving,' said Morris. 'Didn't he tell you? Jack Benton, his manager, was driving when they crashed. Not Cade.'

'But he let Gomez think it was him.'

'Yeah, I noticed that last night. Complex character, isn't he? Heck, we could never have persuaded him to hide out in New Zealand while Jack returned to their place in the States, where we *thought* the main danger was, if he *had* been the driver. It took all Jack's time to talk him into it as it was—they had quite a shouting match at one stage. Jack reckoned Cade was trying to be some knight in shining armour, and carry the can for him, and Cade didn't like that.'

'No, he wouldn't.' Cade prided himself on his toughness, his lack of sentimentality. It seemed to be a necessary defence with him. All the same, in spite of his cynical appraisal of Jack Benton's motives, she believed he was more fond of the man than he would admit—even, perhaps, to himself. Once, in her young ignorance, she had believed she knew Cadiz Fernand. Now she knew that she was only beginning to understand him. But she would never have the opportunity to complete her knowledge of him, to explore the hidden corners of his personality that she had recently glimpsed. He had put up barriers against all women a long time ago, barriers he had no intention of lowering for her. Perhaps, as Morris seemed to think, Carlotta had breached them, a little. She had known him when they were very young, maybe before the barricades had been fully built, and she might have known how to get behind them. Certainly it was true that he was uncharacteristically anxious to help her husband.

Morris cooked them both breakfast, and she managed to steer him away from the subject of last night's events. She found she didn't want to talk about it, any more than she wanted to talk about Cade's imminent departure.

'I have to go to the office,' said Morris as they concluded their meal.

'Can I come?' Carissa asked eagerly, anxious to get away from the apartment, and not to be here alone when Cade returned.

'No. I want you to stay here and entertain Cade when he comes back,' said Morris. 'And don't let him out of your sight. I want a contract signed before he leaves for home. He promised me a tour.'

'I'm sure he won't go back on his word.'

'All the same, I want it in black and white as soon as possible. I'm counting on you, Carrie. Let me know as soon as he gets in, and I'll get back here and make sure I have his signature.'

After he had gone she tidied things up in a desultory

fashion, noticing that the knife had disappeared from
the lounge. She supposed Cade had packed it into one
of his bags.

She wandered into the spare bedroom and saw her
face in the mirror, pale and listless-looking, a droop
to her mouth and faint shadows under her eyes.

Impatient with herself, she sat down and carried out
a full make-up treatment, smoothing tinted foundation
under her eyes to hide the hollow look, using a pink
lipstick, brushing her hair fiercely until it gleamed
softly. When she had finished she looked herself critically over, decided the soft shading of green on her eyelids, the subtly darkened lashes and the faint brush of
blusher on her cheeks were a definite improvement,
and decided to go the whole hog by dressing up to it.

Mostly she had worn casual shirts and slacks at the
lake, but she had packed one uncrushable, softly
gathered blue-green nylon silk dress that turned her
eyes the same colour and made them look mysterious
and soft. She didn't feel soft, but it was quite a
glamorous all-purpose sort of dress, which was why she
had chosen it, and it would help her feel confident and
able to cope with whatever mood Cade was in when he
arrived, she hoped.

So when she finally answered the door to his ring,
she was looking coolly composed and sophisticated. If
her heart skipped a beat or two at the sight of him, tall
and tanned and looking remarkably fit in spite of the
harrowing events of the previous night, it didn't show.

'How did it go?' she asked with just the right amount
of polite interest.

'Okay,' he said, casting an experienced eye over her,
taking in the careful make-up, the elegant dress. 'It
looks as though Gomez will get off lightly, since he's
quite willing to co-operate with the police, now.'

'And since you won't testify against him.'

'That, too.'

He spoke almost absentmindedly, his eyes unreadable but intent on her, making her nervous.

'Did you have breakfast?' she asked.

'Yes, also a cup of tea at the police station, although I think the Inspector would have preferred to give me bread and water.'

'You probably did him out of a promotion.'

'He'll get other opportunities.'

He moved closer to her, and she asked, 'Would you like a drink?'

'Not now. Carissa——'

Trying to look casual, she turned away from him to go to the phone.

'I promised Morris to let him know when you came back.'

He followed her, and as she lifted the receiver he said, 'Not yet. I want to talk to you.'

'I promised,' she said calmly. 'He really wants to see you——'

She had begun to dial when he took the receiver from her hand and replaced it. Because she always reacted strongly, one way or another, to his proximity, the action angered her.

'I said, *not yet*,' he said clearly, close to her ear. 'I'll see Morris later. He'll get his contract.'

'When it suits *you*!'

'That's right.'

She would have pushed past him, but he was leaning one hand with seeming casualness against the wall, trapping her.

'You do like to get your own way,' she said. 'Don't you, Cade?'

'Count on it,' he said mockingly. 'You're angry. Your eyes have gone emerald green. Remember that waiter in Sydney?'

'No.' She turned her face away, trying to look indifferent.

He gave a soft laugh. 'Yes, you do.'

'All right, then, I don't want to. I don't want to be reminded of it. I don't *want* to remember it.'

'None of it?' he asked. 'Not this?' He trailed his lips gently from temple to cheek to the corner of her mouth. 'Or this?' He stemmed her attempt at evasion and pulled her close to kiss her mouth, surely and thoroughly, and she exerted every shred of willpower she could muster to ignore the wild singing in her veins that urged her to respond and never count the cost.

He was only amusing himself, trying a last attempt to salve his vanity and prove his attraction for her, she told herself bitterly as at last his arms slackened and she pushed away from him, turning blindly to move out of the room and on to the small patio, for she felt she needed the mind-clearing effect of fresh cool air.

Cade followed, standing in the doorway as she stood agitatedly plucking pink wisps of blossom from a tamarisk that bloomed in a tub just outside.

'What do you want of me, Carissa?' he asked.

'Nothing that you can give me,' she answered huskily. 'I told you I don't know how to love——'

So he had guessed—guessed at her feelings for him, her longing for the love he was unable to give her. Hurt pride made her round on him, in passionate fury.

'I don't want your love!' she lied desperately. 'I don't want you in any way. Oh, yes'—she added, seeing the scepticism in his dark face—'for a while, at the lake, I admit I was a bit carried away sometimes by —by memories of a teenage crush, mainly, and simple propinquity. But you rather shattered my illusions when you started implying that I wasn't to be trusted. That was the beginning of the end. And now that we're back in normal surroundings, I find I can't wait to see the last of you. You're conceited and arrogant and self-willed. And I can't imagine why you bother with that poor Gomez man, unless you like the image of yourself as the hero and the lordly dispenser of benificent charity and forgiveness!'

That was unfair and unforgivable, she realised, the moment the words left her lips. She would have apologised, but he stopped the words with a harsh laugh.

'Not exactly,' he said. 'It's something much more basic than that!'

Carissa stared, and he went on, 'I'm surprised you haven't worked it out. Supposing I had testified against him and he was sent to jail—maybe for years. He would have come out an even more bitter man than when he went in. The problem would only be postponed, but not solved. This way he's off my back for good, my friend for life. By the way,' he added, 'I must thank you for helping to make him see sense last night. I think it was your sincere little speech that tipped the balance.'

Feeling vaguely sick, she said, 'It *was* sincere. Weren't you? I thought you genuinely wanted to help him.'

'I did. I have a genuine interest in the preservation of life—*my* life.'

'What you told him about Carlotta—was it true?'

Cade paused, his eyes unfathomable, a shuttered look coming over his features. 'Substantially, yes,' he said at last. 'I plead guilty to omitting one or two details. She did ask me for money to get them away from his unsavoury connections and allow him to continue to lead a blameless life. Carlotta had attained respectability at considerable cost, and she wanted to hang on to it. She also was very fond of her husband and their child. As for the rest——' he smiled rather cynically, 'shall we just say that the lady was not quite the paragon of virtue that I let her husband think she was. As a matter of fact——'

'I don't want to hear any more!' she interrupted. 'You told me once you always buy your women. She must have been very beautiful—you seem to have paid a high price for her.'

She pushed past him, ignoring the glittering fury in his eyes, holding her breath as she passed close to him, but no reprisal eventuated. And he just stood where he was as she dialled Morris's number and told him Cade was waiting for him.

She busied herself preparing lunch for them all while they waited for Morris, making a salad and frying some frozen French fries and rissoles. Cade stayed out on the patio, eventually subsiding into the chair that he had been occupying only a few weeks ago when Carissa had come in with Morris to find him waiting. It seemed an age ago, now. So much had happened since then, she felt life would never be the same again.

Fortunately, Morris was too full of talk to notice that Carissa and Cade hardly spoke to each other, and that Carissa was barely capable of speaking at all. She was frankly at screaming point, wanting the day over, wanting Cade to be gone. It would be easier to pick up the pieces once he had flown out of her life. She would resign from her job just as soon as she could without making Morris suspect the reason. Certainly well before Cade returned for his concert tour. Nothing would make her risk going through all this over again.

She cleared the table and Morris spread a contract on the table. Cade seemed to take an age to read it. He took out a pen and scribbled some alterations, and once Morris glanced at her as though he would have liked her opinion. She looked away, not wanting to be asked for it, not wanting anything at all to do with this.

Then it was signed and Morris was folding it up with a satisfied air and putting it in an envelope.

Cade said, 'You can sort out the monetary details with Jack. I'll stay in a hotel tonight. I've an early flight booked in the morning.'

Morris protested but Cade, as usual, got his way.

Carissa booked him a room and he cut short Morris's offer of a car driven by her to pick him up in the morning and take him to the airport.

'I'll get a cab,' Cade said shortly. 'Carissa has had enough of me, this trip.'

Carissa was incapable of making any polite protests, and Morris's hasty assurances that he was sure she wasn't only underlined her silence. He cast her a worried and puzzled glance, then offered to drive Cade to the hotel himself, much to Carissa's relief.

'Do you mind if I go home, Morris?' she asked. 'I'll be in to work tomorrow.'

'Take the day off if you like,' he said. 'You're entitled to some leave.'

'I'm sure she is,' Cade agreed pleasantly. 'She's been —more than you said she was, Morris.'

'We'll drop you off,' said Morris, and Carissa had to endure the drawn-out bittersweet pain of riding in the back seat while the two men chatted in front. Or Morris chatted and Cade replied in, for the most part, polite monosyllables.

When they stopped Cade got out and opened her door for her, but she held her bag firmly, not letting him carry it in.

'I'll manage, thanks,' she said. She put out a hand and said steadily, 'Goodbye, Cade. Good luck.'

He ignored the hand and tipped her chin to drop a brief, hard kiss on her lips. 'Goodbye for now, sweet Carissa,' he said. 'Thanks for—everything.'

She steeled herself not to watch as the car drove away.

CHAPTER NINE

SHE didn't take a day off. She preferred to go to work and try to keep herself too busy to think about Cade.

She kept busy, all right, but it didn't stop her thinking. Morris had acquired a signed picture from Cade before he left, and it had joined the gallery lining the passageway to Morris's office. Every time Carissa passed it the black eyes seemed to gleam mockery at her, and she winced inwardly as she tried to avoid looking at it.

She dragged herself through each day by sheer determination, presenting a smiling if slightly strained face to the world, and although her apartment mate asked once if she was feeling all right, she was able to congratulate herself on fooling most of the people most of the time. But sleepless nights took their toll, and about a month after Cade had departed, Morris took a good look at her one day and said, 'You know, it's time you had a holiday, Carrie. Why don't you take some time off while it's slack? I can handle all we have on over the next two weeks, and the lodge is free, if you'd like to use it. Take a girl friend with you, if you like.'

At the mention of the lodge her fingers tightened on the notebook she was holding. Telling herself not to be ridiculous, she deliberately relaxed them, saying smoothly, 'I'm all right, Morris. The last few weeks have been fairly busy, that's all.'

'No busier than usual. You should have taken a couple of days to relax after that Fernand business, instead of coming back to work. All that must have been a strain for you. That's another thing—we'll have bookings to make for Cade's tour and all the arrangements will have to be finalised in the next month or so. You take a break and I'll get you on to that when you come back——'

'No!'

'What?' Morris looked blank.

'I'm sorry, Morris——' She was being clumsy about this, but it had to come some time. 'I've been thinking. It isn't a holiday I need, it's a change of job. I'm getting a bit—tired of the all constant pressure in this job. I'm—I'm giving you notice, Morris.'

He couldn't have looked more stunned if she had hit him.

'You're—but Carrie, you *can't!*'

'I'm not indispensable,' she smiled. 'You'll find another dogsbody——'

'But you *can't!*' Morris repeated. 'What about the Cadiz Fernand contract?'

Trying to prevent her voice from trembling, she said, 'What about it? Someone else can handle the bookings——'

'No, no, no! Haven't you read it?'

With a sudden chill creeping over her, she said, 'No. I just filed it without looking at it. What difference can it possibly——'

'Look, I don't know what went on between you two at the lodge——'

'Nothing went on, Morris—*nothing!*'

'Okay, I'm sorry—I know you're a girl with principles, Carrie, but that clause in Cade's contract—I guess he made a pass or two and you turned him down, is that it?'

'No comment,' she said coldly. 'What clause in his contract?'

'He wrote it in when you were there,' Morris said unhappily. 'I thought you knew—he wants you on the tour with him. Carissa Martin to accompany him on the tour as my representative. Otherwise, he could cancel.'

Numbly, Carissa stared. *'Why?'*

'How should I know? I thought you did.'

'Well, your new assistant will just have to take my place,' said Carissa. 'He'll have to be satisfied with that.'

'Carrie, you know he won't be. He asked for you by name. It's you he wants.'

It's you he wants. Her mind echoed the words bitterly. For how long? she wondered. A night? The duration of the tour? One thing she knew—Cade's wants were temporary, offering a brief ecstasy and then—heartbreak. For her, it wasn't nearly enough.

'Do you know what you're asking me to do?' she asked.

Morris looked hurt. 'I'm not asking you to do anything against your principles,' he said. 'So, maybe the man's attracted to you, and you don't want to know. You've dealt with the situation before. And surely, if you could handle him at the lodge, when the two of you were alone, you won't have any trouble on tour, with his manager and the band and all the other members of the tour party—heck, you know there's no privacy on tour, except when two people both make good and sure they get it!'

'Morris, I can't! I want to leave!'

'Have you another job lined up?'

'Not yet,' she admitted. 'Not exactly.'

'Well, what difference is a couple of months or so going to make? Take that holiday, Carrie, and do the tour for me, and then maybe you'd like to think about it again.'

'Morris, I really don't think——'

'Carrie, I've got thousands of dollars tied up in this tour, and you know Fernand! I like the guy, but there's no doubt he's a tough customer. You know he'll insist on having everything his way, or no deal. He can afford to back out, Carrie. I can't!'

So Carissa gave in, feeling resentful and upset, and angry with herself because in spite of her knowledge of what it would mean for her, her heart was singing at the thought of seeing Cade, of spending weeks with him on the road.

She went to the lodge because Morris insisted, and she half thought she might lay some ghosts there. But there were too many memories. She lay on the sand and imagined Cade's tanned torso lying beside her, his warm hand pulling her up beside him to race into the water again. In the house she heard the echo of his guitar, his voice softly humming a new song. At night she dreamed of his kisses, his hands on her body, and she woke to stare aching into the morning light while her pulses slowed and bleak reality cooled her heated skin. After four days she packed up and flew to Invercargill to spend the rest of her leave with her brother. It was not entirely successful, since Clive was away at work, but he put her up in his apartment and introduced her to some of his friends, and she went out a lot. It passed the time, and at least it was a long way from Kamahi Lodge.

When she returned to work, Morris looked her over sharply and made no comment on her looks, from which she deduced wryly that they had not improved.

'I stayed with Clive most of the time,' she said defensively. 'He goes round with a fairly lively crowd.'

'You were supposed to be resting,' Morris growled, but he looked vaguely relieved.

'Well, they say a change is as good as ...' she said flippantly. 'Now, what have you got for me today?'

He had plenty, and for the next few weeks she was immersed in work. When it dealt with the Fernand tour she trained herself not to be sensitive about it, and eventually she was able to contemplate his name and the publicity photographs without a visible tremor. Morris was promoting the tour in a big way, making

capital of the fact that personal appearances of Cadiz
Fernand were rare now. He was justifiably proud of
his coup.

She made the hotel bookings, noting that Cade had
stipulated a two-bed suite for himself. So he still preferred to have Jack nearby, even though he was no
longer blind. A third person was to have a single room.

Carissa tried hard to find an excuse not to go to the
airport when Cade finally arrived, but Morris took it
for granted they would both be there, and she was
needed to help organise the arrangements to whisk
Cade off the plane and into the VIP lounge for a brief
television interview and then to his hotel.

The meeting was easier than she had anticipated.
Morris was hastily shaking Cade's hand when the dark
eyes met hers briefly, and she noted he looked lean and
fit and relaxed. She recognised Jack Benton and returned his beaming smile, wondering if he remembered
her without prompting, or if Cade had casually re-
freshed his memory of eight years ago. In spite of herself her face burned a little.

Cade glanced about and smiled at someone standing
a little behind him, putting out a hand to bring her
forward, and Carissa realised that the pretty, dark-
haired young woman who had been hovering nearby
was with him. She had been told to book a suite and a
single room, and had supposed the third person was a
secretary or an assistant for Jack, or simply someone
who looked after the equipment. Now, as she watched
Cade slip his arm about the strange girl, and saw the
quality of the smile she gave him, sweet and a little shy,
her heart began a slow thumping of forboding.

Then Cade transferred his glance to Carissa, still
smiling. 'This is Rita,' he said to her. 'She's shy of
publicity. Look after her for me, will you?'

Carissa wondered if her smile looked as stiff as it
felt. Automatically she put out her hand and felt

smooth, slim fingers touch hers. Then an airport official was leading them all to the lounge, Cade and Morris together, then Jack, with the two women in the rear. Carissa gathered that she was supposed to keep Rita away from the press, so she quietly led her to a secluded corner of the room while Cade conducted the interview.

She supposed she should be making some kind of subdued conversation, but for the moment speech had deserted her. Rita didn't seem to mind. Her gaze was fixed on Cade, with a soft light in her eyes compounded fairly obviously of pride and love. Watching her, Carissa was suddenly shaken by compassion. *Don't love him so much!* she wanted to say. The girl made it so obvious, and Cade wasn't capable of appreciating or returning what Rita had to give.

It wouldn't be any use, of course. Love alighted where it would, and Carissa knew only too well the futility of trying to change its direction once it fixed on Cade. She looked over at him, sitting at ease in a lounging pose, parrying questions with lazy replies that brought an occasional spurt of laughter from the interviewer.

Deliberately, in case her face should betray her as Rita's did, Carissa removed her eyes from Cade and transferred them to the girl. Rita was not as young as she had first thought. There were tiny lines at the corners of her eyes, and her hands had not the smoothness of a young girl's. When she was smiling her mouth had a soft sweetness, but when she moved her gaze from Cade to find a cigarette in her bag, her lips set in a slightly hardened line, and she began to look like someone who had 'been around', perhaps taken some hard knocks in life. In spite of the loose dark hair that framed her face, her casual denim suit, the slim and pretty figure, Rita was not a girl, but a mature woman, probably quite a lot older than herself, Carissa realised.

Now, with the cigarette in her hand, blowing smoke with a practised air, her shapely legs crossed casually at the knee, she looked sophisticated and sure of herself. It was only with Cade, Carissa realised, that the woman became vulnerable.

She was wearing a wedding ring, which gave Carissa a bad moment when she noticed it. She clenched her fingers, remembering the ring that Cade had given her, with the casual information that it was his mother's. Only later, of course, she had realised the reason for his angry indifference to its sentimental value. It hadn't been his mother's at all, but simply a secondhand trinket picked up in a pawnshop by Jack, to go with one of his invented stories about Cadiz Fernand. She wondered if Jack had any idea how much that had hurt Cade—and then she wondered how she knew. But she did. The cynicism he had displayed about it revealed the depth of the hurt. It was Cade's way of covering up.

Had he given a ring equally casually to Rita? Or was the ring some other man's token of love? Cade said Rita was shy of publicity. She didn't really look the type to be embarrassed by the fact that she was travelling with Cade—unless she was, perhaps, still married to someone else ...

Other men's wives—for the first time she wondered if Cade had brought Rita along in order to torment herself. Why else would he have insisted on her coming on the tour, and then casually introduced her to this woman who was surely his current mistress? Had he planned it all simply to hurt her?

Or had he simply met Rita and wanted her along, without giving a thought to the girl in New Zealand whose company he had once wanted enough to write a clause into his contract ensuring she accompanied him on this tour?

She realised that through the cloud of blue smoke from her cigarette, Rita was appraising her with a shrewd look. 'Cade said he spent some time with you when he was here last,' she said.

'Did he?' Carissa said cautiously.

Rita suddenly gave her charming smile. 'He was pretty cagey about it, though. He said you were clever and efficient and cool. Somehow I had the impression you were a bit older and more—well, more the spinster secretary type. I should have known.'

'What should you have known?'

Quite gently, Rita said, 'Am I speaking out of turn? I'm sorry—I haven't been with Cade very long, and I'm curious about him, about what he's been doing, the people he knew before we——'

Jack interrupted her, asking if they were ready to go because the interview was over and they had just an hour and a half to get to the hotel and prepare for a press interview that Morris and Carissa had set up for Cade.

'Cade wants you to go with him,' he told Rita. There were two cars waiting, and Morris, Jack and Carissa shared the second one. Carissa had slipped away from Rita's side as Cade opened the door of the cab, and when he looked around for her she was climbing into the other one with Morris.

She saw him turn and smile at Rita as the car moved off ahead of them, and Jack, getting in and shutting the door beside him, turned and said, 'Cade said he'd write and tell you himself about booking for Rita, too—it's all fixed, is it?'

'Carrie?' Morris queried confidently, and she said, with a hollow feeling inside,

'Yes, Jack. Everything's just as Cade ordered. A suite and a single in each hotel.'

'Good,' said Jack. 'Surprised you, did it? I must admit the whole thing surprises *me*, a bit. You wouldn't believe the difference in that guy since Rita's been with him.'

Carissa would have left it there, allowed Jack to turn and face the view from the windscreen, but Morris was curious. 'How has he changed?' he asked.

'Well——' Jack paused. 'I've known Cade a long time. He's a great guy, a great entertainer—and a good friend. But he's kinda sharp-cornered, you know. When he's in a certain mood, you watch your step.'

'He's tough,' Morris added.

Jack made a deprecatory face, shrugging slightly. 'Yeah—yeah,' he conceded. 'He's a good guy, but he's tough. But, with Rita, it's different. Some of the edges have been taken off. Guess he never had anyone before he really cared about. He hardly lets her out of his sight, you know. You'd think she was made of glass—which she definitely ain't! Our Rita's been around a bit, you know. In fact, I wasn't too keen when he insisted on having her with him—a girl with her background. But he pleased himself, as usual, and I have to eat my words. She's been good for him, and she sure is reformed. In fact, it might make good publicity—it's sort of romantic, Cade finding her working in some sleazy dive like he did. But there's her ex-husband— she doesn't want him to know——' He paused. 'Of course, this is all off the record,' he said. 'Rita's a great girl, I don't want her hurt—and Cade would kill me. You won't use it?'

Morris assured him they wouldn't. The contract meant too much to him to risk losing it.

When the car stopped outside the hotel Carissa said to Morris, 'Do you mind if I go now, Morris? You won't need me again today, and there's heaps to do still before we leave for the tour.'

Reluctantly, he agreed, and she went back to the office to tie up a few loose ends—it wasn't true there was a lot to do, but she managed to occupy herself— and then she went home. There was to be one concert in Auckland the following night, and two more here at the end of the tour, after they had been to the other main centres. The backing group who were local musicians had already put in many hours of rehearsal, and tomorrow they would rehearse with Cade before the first show went on. She had no need to see him to-morrow and—she took two aspirins and lay down on her bed, hand against her throbbing eyes. She couldn't go on tour with him, not now.

Probably he no longer wanted her to, anyway. He had met Rita now and by Jack's account Rita was pretty special. It was rather obvious that none of his other girls had affected him as she did. For once, he cared. She should have been happy for him, for his having at last found love, but instead she felt nothing but a dull anguish. Why couldn't it have been her?

She worked in the office all the next day, finding things to do. She should have been at the concert in the evening, but instead she told Morris she had a head-ache and wanted an early night ready for the begin-ning of the tour the following day. Although by now she had worked out a plan and had no intention of joining the plane they had chartered for Wellington.

She phoned Morris just before the time she should have been meeting him in the morning, and said, 'Morris, I feel rotten. You'll have to send Sandra, or tell Cade he'll have to manage without a dogsbody. Unless you go yourself. I could cope with the office once I get over this—this bug I seem to have picked up.'

'Have you seen a doctor?' Morris asked when he had assimilated the fact that she was telling him she was too sick to go on tour. 'What sort of bug is it? 'Flu?'

'I guess so,' she said cautiously. 'Look, I'm sorry, Morris. I know it's making things awkward for you——'

'Awkward! Cade's going to be——'

'Relieved, probably,' she said rather cuttingly. 'Since he wrote that clause into his contract, things have rather changed.'

'Well, maybe, but I still think he's going to be mad——'

'Let him be,' Carissa said crisply. 'He can't do anything about it, and he certainly can't blame you. I'm sick, and I can't come, and that's that. I'll get back to the office as soon as I can, but no tour.'

She didn't get dressed because if Morris decided that Sandra could be trusted to take her place, he might take it into his head to come round with flowers or fruit for the invalid. She occupied herself brushing her hair after she had showered and put on a flowered cotton brunch coat, and experimenting with different styles, but her fingers were clumsy and in the end she let it hang loose about her shoulders. The clock moved slowly to take-off time, and her nerves were jumpy with tension.

She tidied the apartment and tried flipping through a magazine that her apartment mate had bought the day before, but there was still half an hour to go.

The fridge needed cleaning, she noticed, as she took out some milk to make a cup of tea. Not that she really wanted the tea, but it would fill in a few more minutes.

She made it slowly and drank it, then decided to clean the fridge. With an apron tied over the brunch coat she emptied the contents on to the table, filled a bowl with warm water and got down on her knees to start cleaning the shelves.

When the doorbell rang she stayed there for a few seconds, her eyes flying to the clock on the wall. Take-off time, exactly. She must be safe, now.

She put the bowl on the floor and pulled off the apron, going slowly towards the door and pulling the kitchen one to behind her.

When Cade strode into the flat she must have paled with shock, because he looked at her critically and said,

'Maybe you *are* sick, at that. I didn't believe Morris when he told me.'

'You're supposed to be on the plane!' she exclaimed. 'What are you doing here?'

'I came to fetch you,' he said. ' *You're* supposed to be on the plane, too, remember?'

'But—Morris told you——'

'Yes. When we got to the airport. Did you ask him not to tell me until then that you weren't coming?'

'No.'

'You've got your colour back,' he said. Suddenly moving closer, he put a hand to her forehead, then cupped her chin. ' 'Flu, he said. You don't have a fever, your eyes are clear, your voice is normal. Why don't you want to come?'

'You can't want me to, really——'

'Let *me* decide what I want!'

'How I wish you'd return the favour!' she said bitterly. 'All right, I don't have 'flu. But I don't feel too bright, either.'

'Have you eaten this morning?'

She shook her head. 'I had a cup of tea.'

He looked around, then pushed open the door of the kitchen. 'Is this the kitchen?' He looked back at her, saying, 'I'll make you something,' and must have seen the guilt on her face. He swung round and saw the bowl on the floor, the open door of the refrigerator, the food spread on the bench. 'Do you always decide to spring-clean when you're feeling ill?' he asked bitingly.

'I'm not spring-cleaning,' she said weakly. 'The fridge needed—oh! Leave me alone!'

'I'll clean this up and get you something to eat while you pack,' he said, quietly but implacably. 'You'd better hurry. They're waiting for us.'

After a moment, she obeyed. For some reason he was determined she was going to come, and at the moment she had no fight left in her.

She packed with neat haste, well used to it. Then Cade stood over her while she forced down mouthfuls of a surprisingly good omelette and drank another cup of tea under his watchful eye. As she was sipping it he said, 'Jack said he told you about Rita. I meant to do that myself.'

She shrugged with a show of indifference. 'It doesn't matter. It has nothing to do with me—I only make the bookings.'

He tensed, and she knew she had made him angry again. 'Don't you care?' he asked harshly.

'No.' She put down the cup and got up. 'The trouble with you is, you're too used to having your own way, and too accustomed to having a bevy of adoring women about you. Well, Rita obviously adores you—I should have thought that would be enough. Why must you drag me along on this dreary tour as well?'

His lips thinned, he said, 'For Rita's sake. She's the only woman in the party if you don't come. She needs a feminine companion.'

Carissa blinked, then gave a scornful little laugh. 'Good heavens, you're not telling me a girl of her sort needs a *chaperone*?'

She was totally unprepared for the sudden swing of his hand, the sting of his palm against her cheek.

The blow made her sway and clutch at the table, staring at him from a white face with disbelieving eyes. He looked pale, too, pale and furiously angry, his eyes glittering with temper.

'Say what you please about me,' he snapped. 'But keep your vixen's tongue off Rita, understand?'

She supposed it had been a waspish thing to say. She swallowed, wanting to tell him she hadn't meant it, to apologise. But tears threatened to overwhelm her, and her throat tightened on the words and wouldn't let them out.

Cade ordered, 'Get your things.'

Blindly she turned and went into the bedroom, scribbled a note for her apartment mate and picked up her case. She didn't dare suggest washing the dishes before they went. She would just have to apologise to Cathy for leaving them when she got back.

They sat in total silence in the back of a taxi all the way to the airport, and just before they got out Carissa furtively took a quick peep into her compact mirror. Her cheek still tingled, but it didn't show. She looked a little pale and very composed, and was glad of that.

Morris was there, looking slightly bewildered and a little harassed. He kissed Carissa's cheek as he greeted her, casting a curious glance at the remote cast of Cade's face and whispering to her, 'Are you okay? What's with you two, anyway?'

She tried to smile, but her mouth felt tight. 'Mr Fernand just likes his own way,' she said. 'He's set on that contract being fulfilled to the letter.'

'Look, Carrie, if you're really sick, I'll talk to him,' Morris offered. 'He can't insist—he seems to think you're swinging the lead.'

'It's all right, Morris,' she said wearily. 'He'd insist on calling a doctor, who would say there's nothing wrong with me. And then he'd sue you, or walk out on the tour. Don't worry, I'll survive. Look after the store while I'm gone.'

She left him standing and walked past Cade without looking at him, to board the plane. Morris wasn't the only one looking puzzled and curious. She dared not look at Rita, who must be wondering, surely ...

Jack was sitting by a window, and she sank down beside him, watching Cade usher Rita into a seat. Rita did look perturbed, and Carissa's heart sank as she watched her quick, murmured speech and agitated gestures, and saw the sardonic mockery in the tight smile that accompanied Cade's single, brief reply.

Rita's eyes went huge and hurt and she turned to look
out of the window as the plane shook, roared and began gathering speed down the runway.

Cade really was a selfish, heartless beast, Carissa
thought angrily.

She closed her eyes and pretended to sleep until they
landed at Wellington, sweeping in down the runway
close to the harbour and alighting into the chilling
teeth of a typical Wellington wind.

Their hotel was in Oriental Bay, the crescent-shaped
beach with its steeply rising background of well-
populated hillside reminiscent of Hongkong, and the
rooms had views over the water. There was a photo-
graph in the lobby of the foundering of the *Wahine*,
the ferry which some years ago had sunk in a storm with
the loss of fifty-two lives, while the people of Wellington looked on helplessly from the shore.

'My husband took that photo,' the proprietress told
them with a mixture of pride and remembered horror.
'From one of our windows.'

Carissa looked away, and caught Cade's eyes on her,
hard and speculative. They were taken up to their
rooms, and she took the first single one, longing to get
away from the others. It was as her case was being
sorted out from the rest of the luggage on the baggage
trolley that she saw the label on one of the smart new
blue leather cases that made up a matching set of three.
Rita Franklin.

She took her bag and thanked the man and closed the
door of her room before she allowed herself to take in
the implication.

Rita Franklin, the tag had said. Franklin was the
name Cade used when he wanted to be incognito. Pre-
sumably his real name. As though her mind was trying
to ward off the shattering knowledge, she doggedly pur-
sued each logical step, one at a time. Franklin was
Cade's name. Rita was travelling under Cade's name.

Women who were merely living with a man these days didn't bother to assume his name—and besides, it would be illegal to use a passport with a false name, wouldn't it?

Rita Franklin. Mrs Rita Franklin, of course. They were married. Cade was married.

She unpacked and stowed some of her clothes in the small closet in the corner, then stood at the window, looking out at the grey water, and tried to think of nothing at all. She hardly realised that she was crying until there was a tap on the door, and she turned, hastily wiping tears from her cheeks as Rita opened the door.

The other woman looked concerned. 'Cade sent me to see if you were all right,' she said. 'What's the matter?'

'Nothing,' said Carissa. 'I'm fine really.'

After a moment's silence Rita said, 'Cade can be a bit of a brute, sometimes, even to me. He doesn't seem able to make up his mind if you're really unwell, or just pretending. He went off in a towering rage to fetch you, and he nearly bit my head off, in a nasty, sarcastic way, when I suggested he'd been a bit harsh with you. Most of the time, he's terribly good to me, and I can take his occasional flashes of temper. I had much worse than that from my ex-husband. But you're not as tough as I am——'

'It has nothing to do with Cade,' Carissa lied valiantly. 'I was—I was looking out the window and thinking of the *Wahine*.'

Rita looked sceptical for a moment, then she transferred her gaze to her hands, sitting on the bed as though she meant to stay, and said, 'Oh, yes. The leader of the backing group has just been telling us about it. It was a terrible disaster, wasn't it? Did you know anyone who was on the ship?'

'No. But the news and the papers were full of it for

days—all the details. I was at an impressionable age. Being here, and the picture in the lobby, just brought it all back.'

'Well, there's a bit of a party going on in Cade's suite. We had drinks brought up. Why don't you join us, and cheer yourself up?' Carissa hesitated, and Rita said, 'Come on, honey. Rinse your face and put on some make-up. It'll make you feel better. And maybe Cade won't be quite such a bear, either.' She grimaced, laughing.

Carissa took her advice. It would do no good to remain skulking in her room, and at least there was safety in numbers. She had to face Cade again some time, and it should be easier in a room full of people.

They went into the suite together, and from across a room which seemed full of young men with glasses in their hands, and some with guitars on their knees, as they lounged about the chairs or the floor, Cade looked over at them, and his face softened as he smiled.

That's how he looks for Rita, Carissa told herself painfully, as Rita drew her into the room. Jack and another man got up from a small sofa and the two women sat down side by side, while Jack went to get them drinks.

But it was Cade who brought them over, smiling at Rita, the smile still lingering as he turned to Carissa and murmured, 'Feeling better?'

'Quite a lot, thanks,' she answered, and found her gaze caught and held by his. The enigmatic look was gone, and he seemed to be trying to look into her mind, as though he wanted badly to know what she was thinking.

Then someone called him and he turned away.

The drink warmed her, and she did feel a little less bleak. The group's drummer, a young man she knew slightly, sank down at her feet and began to talk to her while Rita chatted with Jack Benton and another man. Someone began to play the guitar, and several voices joined in singing. The drummer persuaded her to dance, and Rita was pulled to her feet by someone else.

The party broke up with the sound of the dinner gong. In the dining room the drummer pulled out a chair at a table for two and Carissa was glad. He was making a mild play for her, and she didn't mind. Anything that would remove her from Cade's immediate vicinity was welcome just now.

She kept her eyes averted from the table where Rita was seated with Cade and Jack Benton, and tried to concentrate her attention on the young man who was trying to capture it.

She even went to the bar with him afterwards and had a few drinks, sipping them very slowly to make them last. Two other members of the group came in and they sat and talked for a couple of hours before she excused herself, tactfully declining the drummer's offer to accompany her.

She was at the door of her room when Cade's door swung open and he came into the corridor. She hastily turned the handle and was already shutting the door behind her when his striding step brought him to it, and he pushed it wide again, stepping into the room.

'You've been long enough,' he said, as the lock clicked behind him.

'I don't remember inviting you in.'

'I want to talk to you. You seem to have made a remarkable recovery.' Carissa's cheeks were warm from the crowded bar and the three drinks, and her eyes held a sparkle of temper.

'Therapy,' she said sarcastically, remembering the sting of his hand on her cheek this morning, his overbearing tactics to get her on the plane.

But Cade totally misunderstood. 'Oh, yes,' he draw-

led. 'The young drummer—sweet words and handholding.'

There hadn't been any handholding, at least not for
longer than it took her to remove her hand from the
boy's hold when he tried it, but after opening her
mouth indignantly to deny it, she decided the quickest
way to persuade one man she wasn't interested in him
might be to pretend an interest in another. So she
shrugged, and allowed her mouth to curve into a small
smile, and let him think what he liked about that!

It seemed Cade didn't like it much. His mouth went
grim, and he didn't speak for a minute.

Coolly, she enquired, 'Was there some problem with
the arrangements, Mr Fernand?'

His suddenly narrowed eyes should have warned her,
but his hands biting into her shoulders, jerking her
close to him, were totally unexpected. Her gasp of
shock was cut off by his mouth descending cruelly
against her lips, forcing her to part them to a ruthless,
seeking kiss that made the blood pound in her ears.

He was hurting her, and she made a small protesting
sound in her throat, trying to push him away with her
hands against his hard chest.

Cade captured her hands in his, releasing her shoulders, imprisoning her wrists in one hand behind her,
bringing her body even closer to the demanding
warmth and hardness of his. His mouth softened a little
and began moving on hers almost coaxingly, demanding response instead of mute, resentful submission. Her
whole body ached with need, with the desire to forget
everything but Cade's mouth, his hands, the fulfilment
that the pressure of his body against her promised.
Almost imperceptibly, resistance was melting away, she
was pliantly moulded against his hardness, her soft
mouth clinging to his.

She felt his fingers slide down the zip at the back of
her dress, then his hands eased the bodice off her

shoulders. His thumbs lowered the straps of her bra
and his mouth left hers and began kissing her throat
and moving softly over her shoulders.

She wanted him so much, but still her mind bothered
her with thought, with the knowledge that this was
wrong. She moved her hands against him again, wor-
riedly but without conviction. 'Cade,' she whispered.
'Cade—we musn't—what are you doing?'

'Making sure you never *Mr Fernand* me again,' he
muttered, lifting his mouth only an inch from her
throat, so that his breath caressed it warmly as he
spoke. Then he lifted his head and looked into her
eyes, and his were brilliant with passion and a hint
of laughter. 'Call it therapy,' he said, and kissed her
again, his hands on her bared shoulders, slowly moving
over them and down her back. Reluctantly, she pulled
her mouth away and said, 'Cade, was this what you
meant—when you said you wanted to talk?' She wished
she had stuck to just one drink. Her brain was muzzy.

'No.' He kissed her temple and softly trailed his lips
down the curve of her cheek to the corner of her mouth.
'But what the hell ... Every time we talk we fight.' He
kissed her mouth softly, teasingly. His fingers fumbled
with the fastening of her bra, and he murmured, 'I was
going to talk first and make love later, but I think I
prefer this way ...'

She put one hand behind her and captured his
fingers, bringing his hand down to her waist. 'What
were you planning to talk about?' she asked him softly.

'You and me,' he answered, his mouth moving gently
against hers. 'And Rita.'

Her body was burning with sweet desires, but Rita's
name brought a sudden chill, an utter stillness to its
fevered trembling.

'Rita,' she said in a steady, cool little voice. 'Yes.
Perhaps we should have talked about Rita.'

Suddenly she felt very ashamed.

Cade muttered, 'Not now!' And his fingers eluded hers and moved across the skin of her back with purpose. 'The hell with Rita—with everyone.'

But she suddenly wrenched away from him, her face burning with shamed humiliation. How casually he had dismissed his wife, she thought sickly. And how ready she had been to help him betray Rita. 'You're absolutely despicable!' she muttered, her voice low and husky with emotion. Shaking fingers pulled her dress about her, and found her zip.

'Thanks,' said Cade, his face taut with anger. 'A few minutes ago you weren't objecting. Why the sudden attack of virtue?'

She turned away so that he wouldn't see her face, and he gave a soft, exasperated exclamation. Then she sensed him behind her, and went rigid. But he only slid up the zip of her dress the last few inches and said more gently, 'I don't mean to hurt you. I shouldn't have said it. I shouldn't have forced you to come the way I did, but I wanted you with me, and when you didn't turn up, I got mad.'

'You always do, when you don't get your own way,' she said bitterly.

He didn't answer that, but after a moment she felt his hands on her shoulders, and his voice said in her ear, 'When I left here last time, I hoped I could get you out of my system before I got back. That was the plan, and the test was to be having you with me on tour. It was either that or——'

'Or what?' she asked as he hesitated.

'Or somehow make you listen to me, make you—feel the way I do. You told me you'd become indifferent to me when we parted. This morning you said you didn't care——' His hands moved suddenly and turned her to face him. 'But you still feel something for me,' he said. 'You can't deny it—you wanted me just now. As I still want you.'

'Momentarily,' she admitted.

His hands tightened as though he would have liked to shake her. '*Listen!*' he said tensely. 'Forget what I said about passion without love. Or at least believe I've learned something since I tried to make you see things my way. The other thing happened instead—with you, I began to see what love was all about. I discovered feelings I never knew I had. And sometimes that hurt. So I hurt you in turn, because when I'm hurt I lash out —it's an instinct that I'm trying to curb, especially since I found Rita. She's been hurt enough already.'

'Then how can you——'

'I didn't say I'm perfect! I said I try. We're good for each other, Rita and I, we've both been alone too long, with no one to belong to.'

'If she makes you happy,' Carissa whispered with an aching heart, 'I'm glad for you.'

'She does, of course. But she can't give me what it's in your power to give.'

'She loves you——'

'It isn't the same ... You know that. It took me a long time to get round to considering marriage, Carissa— even when I left you, the thought was barely present, although I knew something irrevocable had happened to me. Rita helped to bring things into focus, to make me realise that love is a permanence. It has to be. We've given each other a lot, these last few months, but it isn't enough for me, Carissa. I wasn't ready to say this before, but now I have to. I love you. Want— need—all those things the songs are all about, but most of all, I love you.'

Wide-eyed, she looked at the blaze in his eyes with bewildered pain. 'But, Cade!' she exclaimed. 'It's too late.'

She saw his jaw tighten and the movement in his throat as he swallowed. 'It's too late,' she repeated.

'I'm sorry—you'll have to make do with what Rita can give you.'

Because she wouldn't be a party to hurting Rita, who had been hurt enough. And Cade had no right to expect to have them both. It would make a mess of all their lives, as he should have seen. Even though she couldn't stop loving him, she had to admit he was still a selfish brute.

He dropped his hands from her shoulders and his face was bleak as he turned to go, the light in his eyes deadened. He didn't look at her again before the door clicked behind him.

CHAPTER TEN

IT wasn't difficult to avoid being alone with Cade the next day. He seemed just as anxious as she was not to have to speak to her. He seemed preoccupied and a trifle terse all day, as though he was controlling his temper with an effort, but she never heard him snap or raise his voice.

In the afternoon the men went off for a rehearsal, and Carissa declared her intention of washing her hair.

'I'll set it for you,' Rita offered, and when Carissa demurred, insisted, 'Please—it will give me something to do.'

As Carissa sat before the dressing table in her bedroom, Rita combed out her hair, saying, 'I wanted to be a hairdresser once. That was before I ran away from home and became—something else instead.' She made a face. 'I expect Cade told you about me.'

'Cade hasn't told me anything,' said Carissa. 'Except that you've made him happy. Jack talked a bit, though. Do you mind?'

'Not really. Except for Cade's sake. I'm not proud of what I was, but as Cade says, I was young and hungry and unloved and unwanted. What else was there to do? I wish Johnny had been as understanding.'

'Johnny?'

'My ex-husband. Oh, I guess I should have told him before I married him that I'd been—on the streets. Heavens, he knew I was no virgin. But I never cheated on him—not once. Even after he started beating me up regularly and making sure I had no money in the house, ever.'

'Oh, Rita—why?'

'Because that was the way he was, I guess. Oh, he *said* it was because some guy he met told him about my past, but I think he would have found another excuse anyway. He was that sort. If I hadn't been so desperate to grab some respectability for myself after being treated like dirt for ten years, I probably would have realised he was no catch as a husband. I guess I used him, in a way. So when he turned nasty I figured maybe I'd brought it on myself. But after four years I couldn't stick it any longer. I just walked out in the clothes I was wearing, no money, no nothing. Thank God, at least there were no kids, either.'

'What did you do then?' asked Carissa.

Rita met her eyes briefly in the mirror, put down the comb and began to plug in a blow-dryer. 'Went back to the only business I knew,' she said wryly.

'Was that what you were doing when you—when Cade——?'

'No, thank heaven. I got a little bit of money and found a place to live, not much, but a room—and then I got a job waitressing. It didn't pay much, but I kept my self-respect, what was left of it. I'll always be glad I had a decent job when Cade found me.' She smiled. 'It wasn't a particularly respectable place, mind. I didn't have any references when I was looking for a job, so I couldn't be too choosy. But at least the waitresses weren't expected to be served up to the patrons. It was a respectable job. I told Cade about my less respectable jobs later, when he said he wanted us to be together. I didn't want him to find out from someone else, and besides, it was only fair to give him a chance to change his mind. Men are funny about these things—even those that patronise girls like—I was—they go through the ceiling if their wife or sister—you know?'

'But Cade didn't mind?'

'Mind?' Rita picked up a strand of hair and eyed it

thoughtfully before twirling it in her agile fingers. 'Yes, he minded. But he minded *for* me, not *at* me, if you know what I mean? Anyway,' she said, 'here am I boring you with the story of my life——'

'No, you're not.' But Carissa didn't want to hear any more reminiscences all the same. She was glad for Rita's sake that she had met Cade and was happy after what she had been through. But for her own she wished passionately that they had never met. And she was conscious of a stirring anger against Cade for his disloyalty to Rita, who deserved something better.

There was no getting out of attending the show with Rita. They sat in the seats reserved for them, and when the lights dimmed and a single spot picked out Cade walking on stage with his guitar, to the enthusiastic applause of the expectant audience, Carissa was carried back in time to a similar occasion in Sydney, years ago.

He sang one or two of the same songs, too, but most of them were newer numbers, and towards the end of the evening his eyes seemed to search the auditorium until he found where they were sitting, and he said quietly into the microphone, 'This is a new song—for Rita.'

It was a haunting little song with a simple but memorable melody. The words were really no more than variations on the theme of the two-line chorus: *It's been a long, long time; I'm so glad I've found you now.*

When the last notes died away, the audience applauded madly, but Carissa's hands were tightly clasped in her lap, and Rita was wiping away tears, but smiling at the same time.

Then Cade was speaking again. 'This one,' he said, 'is even more new. Very new.' He paused. 'It's for another girl——' The audience laughed, but Cade gave no answering smile. 'It's called, *Goodbye, Darling Deceiver.*'

Carissa knew he was singing to her, that this was his way of telling her it was all over. Her throat ached with the effort not to cry as she watched him, his fingers softly stroked the guitar strings, and bitter-sweet words of love and farewell drifted into the dark-ness beyond the spotlight ... *So you're leaving me—but I still love you—my darling deceiver.*

Rita and Carissa were expected backstage after the performance. Carissa hung back as Rita wriggled through the crowd surrounding Cade, and put her arms around his neck to kiss his cheek. 'Thank you for my song,' she said. 'It's beautiful.'

Carissa looked away, and found Jack Benton nearby, staring at her with a puzzled look on his face. He came over to her and said quietly, 'Did you turn Cade down, or something?'

Of course, Jack had unearthed that odd meaning of her name. He must know the song was meant for her.

Carissa tried to smile. 'Don't be silly, Jack. He just used my name to build a song, that's all. He sang one for Rita, too.'

'Oh, sure. But a different kind of song——'

'A love song.'

'Well, that's how the public will sing it, of course, a boy–girl lyric. But you know it wasn't a love song—not like the one he sang for you.'

'I don't see the difference—except that one was hello and the other—goodbye.'

'Well, of course there's a difference, when you know Rita's his *sister*—I mean, that's the difference, isn't it? Look, did you have to turn him down? He's not per-fect, but he's been a good brother to Rita since he found her again—he's changed, I told you that. He would be a good husband—— Are you all right?'

Carissa had hardly heard anything since that single word, *sister*. The room seemed to contract about her and expand again. She felt a little dizzy, dazed.

'But I didn't know,' she said. 'No one told me.'

Jack stared uncomprehendingly. 'Told you what?'

'That Rita was Cade's sister.'

'But you said he'd written and told you about her.'

'No, I said he'd asked us to book for her. He didn't even say it was a woman we were to book for. Just—the number of rooms.'

'But I told you all about her——'

'Yes, except who she was. And I think Cade thought you *had* told us all about her, in the cab from the airport. He asked me if you had, and I said yes.'

'So who did you think she was?'

'His wife. When I found out what her name was.'

'And before that, you thought——' Jack looked knowing.

'Oh, Jack!' she said, remembering. 'I've thought—I've said some appalling things to Cade.'

'Then you'd better unsay them.'

'I couldn't begin to ...'

'Do you love him?'

She didn't answer, looking across the room at the dark head bent to hear something Rita was saying.

His eyes on her face, Jack cleared his throat and said, 'And he's just told the whole world he loves you. Leave it to me.'

He miraculously found her a place to sit, and within fifteen minutes the room was cleared, the band had left, and Jack had hustled Rita into a taxi and left Cade and Carissa to share another.

It was a mild night. The day had been crisp but sunny and there were hazy stars in the sky, and the harbour was hung about with the lights on the crescent shore.

They didn't speak as the car drove smoothly round the harbour. Carissa glanced at Cade's remote profile, that told her nothing, and at the back of the driver's head, and wondered where to start. Jack had manoeuvred them together and then left them to it. But how did one go about trying to sort out such a tangle as she had made?

Cade stopped the taxi before they reached the hotel, and she got out without protest when he opened the door and held it for her.

He turned her towards the beach. She had brought a warm woolly jacket, but her shoes were hardly suitable for beach walking. She stumbled on to the silvery sand, and his hand came out to grip her arm and steady her, only to fall away immediately.

'I'm assuming Jack wouldn't have been able to arrange this if you hadn't been willing,' said Cade.

'No. I—did want to talk to you.'

'About what?'

'You—and me—and Rita,' she said, echoing his own words of the day before.

He stopped walking and turned to her. 'I seem to remember,' he said, 'that Rita is a subject that got us into a lot of strife yesterday—and before.'

'That was—before,' she said. 'Before I found out that Rita was your sister. I thought she was your wife, Cade.'

He was silent for fully half a minute, seeming almost stunned.

'My—*wife*!' he said slowly, at last. 'What on earth made you think that?'

She explained, and he listened in apparent disbelief at first, then finally exploded. 'Of all the *stupid* misunderstandings! I didn't want to put it in a letter, but I thought you'd be pleased I'd located Rita. I wanted to tell you myself all about it, and when Jack got in first I was annoyed. I'd told him I'd do it, but I suppose when you said you'd heard from me, he assumed I'd given you the news.'

'That seems to be it,' she agreed.

He was looking at her keenly, and she thought she knew what he was thinking of—yesterday, and the cross-purposes they must have been at then. Suddenly shy, she asked, 'How *did* you find Rita, exactly?'

'Through Gomez. His daughter was named Rita, and I asked him if it had any connection with the childhood friendship between his wife and my sister. It turned out that they'd kept in touch for a few years, with very occasional letters. That was enough for a private detective to start working on the case, and eventually he traced her. I had advertised, too, but she —she thought I might not want to know her.' His voice had roughened, and she said gently:

'It wasn't true what you told me about only helping Gomez to save your skin, was it? It really was for Rita's sake, all along.'

'I could never quite forget I had a sister,' he said. 'I never managed to stop wondering what she was doing, whether she was okay. I guess I had some twisted idea that if I helped Carlotta out, someone might do the same for Rita, one day, if she needed it.'

'Why did you tell me Carlotta wasn't—as virtuous as you let her husband think?'

'Because I was trying to hurt you—to get a reaction that would tell me if you really hated me, or were covering up for something else.'

'Then it wasn't true?'

'She wanted money badly. She offered me—whatever I wanted in return. And it wasn't the first time she'd sold herself to a man. There was no need to tell Gomez that.'

Carissa felt cold and sick. 'I see,' she said flatly.

His hands suddenly gripped her arms, his voice was savage. 'No, you don't see!' he gritted. 'As a matter of fact, I turned down her offer and gave her the money, anyway. That surprises you, doesn't it? You think I can't walk past a pretty woman without grabbing her and dragging her into my bed! Well, I walked past that one. She had been beautiful once, but worry and lack of money do spoil a woman's looks. I didn't find her all that attractive, so I didn't sleep with her!'

'Cade, stop it!' she cried. 'I'm sorry——'

He dropped his hands and turned abruptly away from her, staring across the dark, moon-dusted water.

She watched him, for a few minutes, then moved to put her hand on his arm. 'I don't think that of you,' she said. 'But—oh, Cade! How you do lash out. You told me you were trying to change.'

She felt his arm stiffen, and then he turned and pulled her close.

'Yes, I do,' he said. 'And I am.' His lips touched her cheek lightly and she wondered if he remembered slapping her. 'I told you a lot of other things too,' he said. 'Do I have to repeat them all?'

'Like what?'

'Like—I love you. And I want to marry you——' His head suddenly came up and he stared at her. 'How could you think Rita was my wife, when I was talking of marrying *you*?'

'But you didn't!' she protested. 'You said when you met me you began thinking of love—and then *Rita* made you consider marriage!'

'Did I? Yes, I suppose I did say something like that. Well, don't misunderstand this, my darling. I want *you* to be my wife. Will you?'

'Yes. Yes, Cade.'

He made her wait for his kiss, looking down at the pale hair falling over wool-covered shoulders, the shining eyes, darkly mysterious in the moonlight, then bending his head slowly as though savouring the anticipation before their lips met and eagerly parted. His hands moved beneath the jacket, replacing its neutral warmth with passionate caresses, but when the jacket slipped and bared her shoulders to his seeking mouth, she shivered in the cool air.

Thickly, he said, 'You're cold, darling. We'll go back

to the hotel. And this time there'll be no fighting.'

She stood in silence as he pulled the jacket about her and looked down at her, her head bent so that she wasn't looking at him. His hands cupped her face and turned it up to him, his eyes narrowed and glinting.

Percipiently, he said, 'You'd rather wait, wouldn't you? You want to be married first.'

Hesitantly, she said, 'Is that silly? When we've already——? It isn't that I don't trust you, Cade, please don't think that.'

'What is it, then?'

'I suppose—when I was seventeen, I thought my parents' values were old-fashioned, that I knew better. But the truth is, I've never felt it was right, what I did then. Perhaps because it happened for all the wrong reasons.'

'Mine were more wrong than yours. At least you only wanted to give—if not love, at least the nearest you were capable of at the time.'

'What did *you* want, Cade? You said "a girl for the night", but was it true?'

'Not quite. Any girl wouldn't have done—I wanted you, yes. But I would have waited if there'd been time. We seemed so short of time, and I wanted some way of holding you, of making you remember me, until I could get in touch with you again. I meant to get your address and somehow see you again—even make a flying visit to New Zealand before we went home after the tour. Then when I found out how young you were, it all became impossible.'

'And so did you,' she said, with a hint of laughter. 'You were so furious——'

'I must have scared you silly,' he said.

'No. And anyway, you softened at the end. You were kind when you said goodbye.'

'And you cried.'

'I've been crying ever since—until now.'

'I can't promise never to make you cry again—you know I'm a bad-tempered, spoiled, temperamental type. But you must promise not to let me get away with it. You've only to look at me softly with those hurt green eyes and I'll be on my knees begging forgiveness.'

Carissa laughed. 'That's not true and you know it.'

He pulled her into his arms and kissed her fiercely. Then his hands smoothed her hair as he muttered, 'Are you going to make me wait?'

'No.'

He looked at her and said, 'You witch! You know damn well I'm going to, because that's what you want. How soon can we be married in this country?'

'I'm not sure. But it can't be too soon for me.'

'Nor me,' he said, with a hint of grimness.

'Oh, Cade——'

'All right,' he said more gently. 'Whatever happened eight years ago, it was to two other people. We start here, and we start right. This time, for you, it's going to be perfect.'

'Yes, it will be,' she said. 'I know.'